Fragmented

JEREMY WORMAN

CinnamonPress

INDEPENDENT INNOVATIVE INTERNATIONAL

Published by Cinnamon Press, Meirion House, Tanygrisiau,
Blaenau Ffestiniog, Gwynedd LL41 3SU
www.cinnamonpress.com

The right of Jeremy Worman to be identified as author of
this work has been asserted by him in accordance with the
Copyright, Designs and Patent Act, 1988. © 2011 Jeremy
Worman,. ISBN 978-1-907090-34-9
British Library Cataloguing in Publication Data. A CIP
record for this book can be obtained from the British
Library.

Designed and typeset in Garamond by Cinnamon Press.
Cover design by Jan Fortune-Wood from detail of original
artwork 'London Bus' © microstock agency. Agency
dreamtime.com
Cinnamon Press is represented by Inpress and by the Welsh
Books Council in Wales. Printed in Poland

The publisher acknowledges support from Arts Council
England Grants for the Arts

LOTTERY FUNDED

London is like a newspaper. Everything is there, and everything is disconnected. There is every kind of person in some houses; but there is no more connection between the houses than between the neighbours in the lists of 'births, marriages, and deaths.' As we change from the broad leader to the squalid police-report, we pass a corner and we are in a changed world. This is advantageous to Mr Dickens's genius. His memory is full of instances of old buildings and curious people, and he does not care to piece them together. On the contrary, each scene, to his mind, is a separate scene, – each street a separate street.

—Walter Bagehot, 'Charles Dickens' (1858)

I may say that up to this time I have been crushed under a sense of the mere magnitude of London – its inconceivable immensity. The place sits on you, broods on you, stamps on you.

—Henry James, letter to his sister (1869)

Contents

Openings

Stolen Dreams (1970s)

Repairs (1990s)

Home Match (2000 and beyond)

Beginnings

To Barbara Hardy

Openings

To the Candyman

He was the only murder victim I ever knew.
I cannot recall his real name, if ever I knew it, but after thirty-five years images of him sometimes fill my mind. We called him the candyman.

He sold high-quality cannabis, and only to people he liked, and never ripped you off: 'For you I will, man, yeah. Come and buy whenever you want,' he said to me during our first conversation in The Railway Arms in Hornsey Rise, a pub popular with squatters. His sense of innocence beguiled you. His withered left arm added to his vulnerability.

A few days later I went to see him. A silver needle glinted from the corner of an unlit stairwell of his block. I knocked on his top-floor flat at 171 Tenby House; I remember the number. No one answered, but 'Mr Tambourine Man' floated out of a cracked window, and it sounded like a lament. Locks clunked, squeaking bolts were pushed back. I brushed the collar of my brown suede jacket before the door opened.

'So you came.'

He smiled sweetly, and the smell of incense poured from his flat: I was welcomed into a phantasmagoric seminary. An entrance hall led to a door, in front of which a red plush curtain slid smoothly on its brass rails. On one side of the corridor three mauve velvet curtains formed cubicles like confessionals.

'They're my meditation areas,' he said.

He took me into the living room. Another door led off from it, which he opened, and I saw a half-dressed young woman laying on three enormous cushions.

'Hello,' she said, 'I'm Janey.' She stood up. 'Got to go now.' She smiled and did up the buttons of her summery dress. I mumbled apologies and she said in a relaxed way, 'He's been giving me advice.' She pecked him on the cheek. He waved her out.

The candyman was not prepossessing to look at: about five feet four inches tall, long mousy hair, round National Health specs; his checked cowboy coat smelt of fried breakfasts; his blue jeans were shapeless. He looked like a damaged scarecrow but his smile was radiant.

There was an energy, a mood about him, which I have never known in anyone else. When he danced in the pub he was as fleet as a leprechaun, his bad arm jigging on its own like an anarchic totem pole, and his shaman-like movements drawing you into a magic arc.

After Janey left he said, 'Let's 'ave a joint, show yer what I've got.' He patted my shoulder and whispered, 'Thanks for coming. We've all got to stick together if the vision thing is goin' to 'appen.' The aura of innocence allowed him to get away with such hippy-dippy talk.

His smile was a glorious thing. It expressed the emblems he revered – the Isle of Wight Festival, San Francisco, Martin Luther King, Gandhi, Jefferson Airplane – as if they were all Free Lovers and Free Love was the natural state of humanity.

With his five wizard fingers he pulled a Sun Valley pouch from his back pocket, and rolled a perfect joint. 'For you, man.' Always courteous, he gave it to me to light. 'It's Leb,' he said, 'really, really good – that'll change yer vision, polish your lenses.' After smoking his dope the pavements did turn gold and the stars did look like dreams you could touch.

The afternoon became soft and blissful, and the winter sun sent shadows across the clear day. My body felt sweet and supple. Time passed. Evening slipped through the window. Our conversation spanned the universe.

A milk bottle smashed on the landing: 'You fuckin' said today!' a stranger's guttural voice shouted as the candyman opened the door. I jumped up and listened.

'It'll be 'ere soon Johnnie,' I heard the candyman say calmly.

I stood in solidarity behind him and said 'Hello' to the stranger.

Johnnie was tall, thin, with the wizened face of a speed freak. He placed his spindly hands on the candyman's shoulder, 'I'll be back tonight,' he shouted. The candyman nodded and said, 'Fine, man, that's fine.' Johnnie's black motorcycle jacket smelt dank.

In the kitchen he made camomile tea and said, 'I owe 'im a favour, that's all, nuffin' to worry about.'

It seemed worrying to me, but I kept quiet, stayed for another hour, bought some Lebanese, and left.

That evening in my flat, as I got stuck into my buckwheat spaghetti and tamari sauce, I tried to work out who Johnnie was.

The next morning I woke sweating after a nightmare about Johnnie, dressed quickly, and ran over to the candyman's flat. He opened the door wearing a red silk spotted dressing gown which came down to his feet: 'Come for breakfast?' he said. 'Very nice.'

I sipped peppermint tea, felt too embarrassed to explain why I was there, but he said 'Johnnie's no bother, 'e's gone, e's happy.' I laughed nervously. I was about to leave when he said he wanted to show me something. From a corner cupboard in his living room he pulled out a crumpled Moroccan-leather wallet and tenderly handed me a torn at the edges, black and white photograph of a woman playing a piano in a village hall. 'Light Classical she called it – I was fourteen when Mum died – the music went on. She's my visshon, man.' He held the photograph up to his nose and sniffed. The claws of his withered arm uncurled. 'We had an allotment, Welwyn

Garden City, she taught me 'bout cuttings and fruit trees, plantin' at the right time.'

When I got back to my flat I burst into tears.

Over the next month the candyman was gone for days on end. When I saw him he was always carrying an army rucksack over his shoulders. On a wet and windy February evening I decided to ask him if he fancied going to the pub. I bundled up into my warmest clothes and slipped a pack of tarot cards into my pocket so I could do a reading for him.

'This way...' – 'Over there...' – 'Hurry up....' In the entrance to Tenby House policemen were running around, shouting orders. There were at least three patrol cars, two police wagons, all with lights flashing.

I sneaked past and began climbing the stairs when a policeman shouted, 'Stop him!' and a scowling young policeman grabbed my arm. I asked him what the problem was and he took a few steps back as my accent gained me brief authority.

'Out the way!' Two ambulance men said as they came down with a stretcher. The candyman's face was covered with a sheet but a turned-up right hand was dangling on the ground. I told the policeman I knew who it was, and gave him my details, as if I was part of a film.

An hour later a man stood on my doorstep: 'I'm Detective Sergeant Reeves.' His thinning dark hair was held down with Brylcreem. His eyebrows rolled as he took in the dinginess. We sat on the window seat. I found I was shaking as I told him about the candyman. I remember catching odd words and phrases as if my consciousness was trying to repel what he was telling me: 'Had no mother...brought up by Dr Barnardo's...£2000 under the floorboards...heroin...big dealer....'

I put my head in my hands and he advised me in a kindly tone to get out of this place. 'It's not for you, son,' he said. I recall looking out of the window at that moment: the sun flashed shadows of almost-leafless plane trees across the flats, the chaos of branches were thin arms.

As far as I know the murder of the candyman was never solved.

Lies, Fiction, Truth:
My Acquaintance with Alan Ross

My first printed story, 'Simon Carver Looks at Life', a
dark tale about a prep school boy and cricket, appeared in
the October/November 1996 issue of *The London
Magazine*. This should have been a happy start to my
belated writing career except that I had lied to Alan Ross
about myself. It was a fertile lie, which forced me to
reappraise myself radically, during a time of mental
exhaustion.

Alan Ross, who throughout his life also suffered from
crippling bouts of depression, had phoned me, sometime
in August 1996, to get biographical details. He was
renowned for being curt on the phone, and I found him
intimidating and slightly grand in his manner. Initially I
was straightforward with him, although he asked a
number of probing questions – he had been in Naval
Intelligence. Then he asked me which school I had been
to, and I tried to sidestep the question by saying that I
had been to Haileybury prep school, and briefly to public
school. Then I talked quickly about my time at a tutorial
college in Windsor, the Polytechnic of North London,
Birkbeck College and Cambridge University.

'Yes, but which school did you go to?'

'Haileybury,' I blurted out, 'but I was only there for a
year or so.'

'Which house were you in?'

'Edmonstone.'

The interrogation over, he told me my story would
appear soon, and we said a clipped goodbye.

In fact I had run away three times in my first term at
Haileybury in 1968 and never went back. I returned

instead to my alcoholic parents in Egham, Surrey, my mother vivacious and violent, my father benign and in the early stages of dementia.

After my first two weeks at Haileybury, I had no intention of staying. I do not believe it was anything to do with the school. The previous school holiday had determined my fate. My father was failing in mind and body, my mother was often drunk and also involved in a messy relationship with my father's chauffeur. Her mood swings, from most loving mother to Lady Dracula, were terrifying. But I was sure that if I were at home I could help my mother and make everything better.

My initial half-truth to Alan Ross was understandable, as I did not wish to dig up these things. I just hoped that he would not use the Haileybury detail in the contributors' notes, but he did – perhaps because, ironically, he was himself an Old Haileyburian. After this I met him briefly on two occasions at his funny little hut of an office in Thurloe Place SW7, but I never mentioned my lie. I brooded on it, and in the spring of 1998 I wrote him a letter revealing the truth. He probably knew anyway as he had connections with the old-boy network.

But that lie showed to me the need I had to cling to some fictionalized idea of myself, and how I still erased the painful, or what I interpreted as most shameful, parts of my life.

My father died in 1970. My mother went on a world cruise and I stayed in Egham. Mrs Dent came in to cook my meals and to keep the house clean. I had my first intense sexual relationship, with the gorgeous Virginia, which cheered me up no end.

From this point on my life was a series of vignettes, lacking connection and purpose: dropping out in Wales; a philosophy degree at the Polytechnic of North London; squatting; involvement with performance-art;

chauffeuring an eccentric barrister in his Rolls-Royce; teaching adult education in the East End; getting a First in English from Birkbeck after four years of part-time study. In 1987 I found myself doing research in Cambridge, and I soon began to supervise students at Peterhouse. Some years later, the Cambridge examiners 'referred' my PhD thesis (meaning that I had more work to do on it) and I accepted an M.Litt.

I had already begun to teach American undergraduates in various colleges in London and in 1994 I was in America on a promotional tour with the American director of one of these colleges. We were driving from Chicago to Galesburg on a long, bleak Midwest road, when I suddenly decided I could not go on. I took the train back to Chicago, then a plane to England and six months of free psychotherapy, courtesy of Tonic, the charity supported by Mike Oldfield.

After this I began to write seriously. At first the autobiographical element was dominant but began to play a smaller part. I believe it was Robert McCrum who said recently in *The Observer* that writing a novel is perhaps the most probing form of psychoanalysis there is.

I am now far happier and living in Hackney with my wife, Nicola, head teacher of a large primary school, and our ten-year-old daughter, Myfanwy. I continue to teach English literature to American undergraduates at Birkbeck. I am writing another novel. My short stories, poems and reviews have been published widely.

In *After Pusan* (1995), the third book of Alan Ross's autobiography, he wrote with directness about his 'present self, emerging shakily from the wreckage of breakdown and depression, cut wrists and crisis'. My sufferings have not been on this scale. I feel that the surface of life is never quite stable.

My lie to Alan Ross was a turning point. He printed two more of my stories. Over the years, he also sent me a

16

number of witty postcards about my stories and reviews or other things. He was a man of great sensitivity and dry humour.

William Boyd, whose first short story was published by Ross, wrote many years later in the *Evening Standard*, that *The London Magazine* is 'a fantastic magazine whose place in the history of twentieth-century literary life grows ever more secure and significant'.

At the time of his death Alan Ross was in a state of severe depression.

Mother's Hats

London was the Mecca of hats for my mother and a shopping trip with her meant something for me too. Our last outing together to 'Town', as Mother called it, was in the late 1960s. We walked the short distance from our house in Egham to the station, a pillbox hat at a tilt on her newly done hair, the seams of her stockings ruler-straight. She strode ahead like a pretty soldier at the start of a campaign.

On days like this it was as if nothing was wrong, as if my mother did not scare me almost to death with her violent outbursts, both physical and mental. We never spoke of this and the silence was like the locked door to a dungeon; if you dared to open it, Mother would push you down the steps into the darkness.

The week before our day out, on a Sunday afternoon, she was drunk in her bedroom. Father was asleep in his room.

'For goodness sake stop drinking, can't you!' I yelled at her.

Half-dressed, she stumbled off the bed. Her right hand jerked out at me, and she raised her first and little finger like the horns of the devil.

'Stop drinking, please. Please,' I cried.

She shouted, 'You pathetic little boy!'

There was an old figurine of a boy and a dog on the side-table. She sort of strangled it in her hands, then hurled it against the wall. The fragile china smashed, the body of the dog and the head of the boy in separate pieces on the floor. That was last week.

We reached the station entrance. 'Mustn't miss the 10.10,' she said cheerily. Her Blue Grass perfume embraced me and I ran like a puppy to catch her up.

The train click-clicked across the nowhere land between Staines and Clapham Junction. 'You're very quiet, darling.' She stared at me through the short veil of her hat. The train arrived at Waterloo. 'Do you see that, darling?' Mother pointed to a well-dressed woman on the platform. 'There could be birds nesting in that hat, looks very dangerous.' The first joke of the day lifted the barrier between us. Then the swirl of platforms and guards, the smell of trains, whistles, and that Waterloo whiff. I squeezed her doeskin-gloved hand. Perhaps this mother would stay and the other one would never return. Perhaps if I loved her more, I could heal her? At the taxi rank she raised her arm and we were off.

I sat on the flip seat and examined her: the beige hat was cube shaped, with a grey circle on top; the light grey two-piece was discreet, with bold stripes of red; grey and black co-respondent shoes; a small black patent-leather handbag. She created a kind of perfection. At times like this I wished my father could come out with us. But he was too ill with a mild form of arteriosclerosis, and he was an alcoholic too, albeit a gentle one. No one spoke about that second illness, which should have been put first. These were Home Counties secrets, hidden where no social worker would dare to pry.

I adjusted my psychedelic pink kipper tie that we had bought at Carnaby Kids last summer. We caught each other's eyes and I prayed I could hold that look, and that love, forever. *You can read a woman by her hats.* I heard Aunt Emily's voice in my head. Not this one. So we played our dressing-up games and became, as we looked to the world, the perfect mother and son, a handsome couple.

Mother wanted something 'really special for Ascot' as she put it, and then said more loudly, so the taxi driver, who had flattered her already, could hear, 'Brims are in this year, big brims, with swirly, bandy stuff all round.' I knew that we weren't that upper class, and with father having to stop work, our income had declined. But Mother's circle of friends was wide, and we mixed with some county people, who took to her with enthusiasm. Now one of them had invited Mother to join her in a box at Ascot.

My dark mood lifted as she bantered with the taxi driver. I said to her, 'My cover drive has really come on since Bulmer gave me a few tips. Will you come and watch me play again?' She smiled. Days out with Mother were better in performance mode. A 'something special' hat was Fortnums or Simpsons. More everyday was Swan and Edgar or John Lewis. 'Country hats', I forget exactly how they were different, meant Aquascutum.

The taxi took us across the Thames, where an old anchored battleship had its guns pointed towards us. Further on, the soft greyness of the London streets made the shops bright. Shadows stretched up a narrow road near Holborn, a tramp was squatting in a doorway. He gulped from a quarter-bottle of whisky. His resigned face reminded me of my father.

Outside Fortnums the doorman smiled broadly and shared a joke with Mother as she pressed a coin into his hand. I loved these moments when our class position was recognised. It made me secure – all pain could be forgotten – and the symbols of our status, and our complicit belief in them, made us invulnerable.

'Have a lovely day, madam', said the doorman. 'Are you going somewhere nice for lunch?'

'Veraswamy's perhaps,' Mother replied, smiling back.

She walked up the stairs and her pillbox hat bobbed like the movement of a girl's bottom trotting on a horse. I followed at a respectful distance, and almost forgot who she was. I felt floaty, high up in bubbly clouds. Then I remembered. You bitch, I thought, you fucking selfish bitch and it was the first blood-red anger I had ever felt for her. I was horrified. I imagined strangling her, or pulling her back down the stairs and screaming: 'How dare you treat me like that? How dare you behave so horribly when you're drunk?' I did not, of course. But planted in my mind was hate that threatened to overcome my unquenchable love and need.

I practised a few forward-defensive strokes to restore my equilibrium. We entered the cool space of the hat department. Mother used to say that the place was 'always full of old dowagers', and last year she had chatted to a real live one, trying on hats next to her, who gave us afternoon tea in the Fountain Room. The old lady dolloped clotted cream onto her scone and enquired about my school, 'He's there, is he?' she purred to my mother. I was not as I had run away in my first term but Mother and I lied so instinctively that no one would have known. Our social double act was so smooth that we could have become a good team of fraudsters. I learnt from Mother, as I watched and copied, that charm could get you most things. The old dame gave mother her phone number and wanted us to visit her in Gloucestershire. 'I haven't ridden for years,' Mother said, 'but I should love to.'

I sat behind Mother as she tried on hats, and avoided her eyes in the mirror. The back of her head had no pull over me. But not to be within the sphere of her aura felt empty. I saw her dressing room at home, which was like a cocoon. There were layers of shelves all round: shoes at the bottom, then a shelf for bags, then one for jumpers and scarves. The top shelf was devoted to hats, in boxes of every style and shape, colour and size.

As you walked in, the hat of the moment was in front of you. Around the time of the shopping expedition, it was a beautifully boxed hat from Saks on Fifth Avenue in New York, 'A cloche hat, darling, an utterly perfect American Thirties-style cloche hat.' She clapped her hands together. 'Just so *you* for that boring old bishop's

21

garden party....' A male friend had bought it for her last spring. The party was being given by a rural dean, and she had been invited because my father had advised our parish church about rateable values, and not charged anything.

I would sometimes be summoned in to her dressing room to inspect a hat, or a new outfit, and the door would shut. I became no particular age, and no particular person. The place was a lavender-scented cave.

A pretty Fortnum's shop assistant, with blonde hair and breasts that strained the buttons of her thin blouse, held out another hat. 'Do you like it, darling?' Mother asked me. 'Darling!'

Mother's eyes caught mine in the mirror. 'Well,' I mumbled, 'don't know.' I wrenched my eyes away and I was in the 'hate field' again, and all her finery peeled off. I saw a witch, who could wear as many faces as she wished. Her different looks could make you 'this' one day, 'that' another, and then sometimes nothing at all. Beneath her ego were the flesh and fibres that made her and would one day become a skeleton, when I would be free from her love-and-hate field. The hat she was trying on was propped on a skinless head of bones.

Nothing could be trusted. The massive window at the end of the shop opened on to the grey-white world beyond where only the sky showed and there were no people. I rushed across the sales floor and my idea was not to stop but to jump out.

Staring down at Piccadilly I tried to connect the few bits of London I knew, but nothing linked up. From the other side of the sales floor I felt Mother's eyes staring at me. I walked quickly round the edge of the shop, down the stairs and out into the street.

Oysters

For two please, I say, my friend will be here any moment and I feel good as I forget the old hippy I was, but no longer am in my one good suit, shining cufflinks, silk tie, polished shoes.

Yes, at the bar is fine. I sit amongst the Savile Row suits and a glass of champagne please I say before I know I have said it.

I sip the champagne, savour the bubbles, and hear the briny crack of oysters as they are opened miraculously at the bar by a man with flashing tentacles for hands. The oysters find themselves on plates with ice, bread and butter, Tabasco and lemon, on their short journeys to the deeps of their customers' guts.

Ah, Elie, I say, sit down. It's great to see him, with his bald dome, youthful face and round tortoiseshell glasses. He looks every inch the successful French publisher.

A bottle of house champagne please! And Elie says, let me! No, I say, this is on me, my treat, please. The old hippy in me winces as this other me speaks as if one does this every day and twice on a Friday.

Our oysters come slurping in their wicked marine juices, alive and plump in their dark-silver mineral shells. The champagne slips down my gullet like liquid velvet. I imagine each bubble in my throat as a tiny £ sign and my pleasure increases because I have consumed so much. Elie says, Look, sorry it didn't work out but when you write the next novel, I'll try again, Paris is so....

His elbows are together on the table, and he opens his hands slowly like a fan. His insouciance irritates me, as if this gesture swims in the Parisian swell of good eating. But the first tender oyster tickles my tonsils with the essence of sea life: Elie, my friend, and I laugh.

I find myself smiling at the pretty Thai waitress; after the fourth oyster I smile again and do you know she smiles back, but which me is she smiling at? Anyway, after the sixth oyster and third glass of champagne she is definitely smiling at one of me and who cares which? More oysters please! I command. I am a secret agent penetrating the very bivalve core of the establishment.

Non, Elie, says, non. Je les acheterai, I insist!

No, no, Elie. J'insiste!

And I do and he *does* buy the second bottle of champagne and it's only Wednesday. I wish there were someone at home to benefit from my tumescent love – perhaps the gorgeous waitress? She probably thinks I'm one of them. Little do you know, my dark angel.

By the tenth oyster *I am* one of them: from here I will take the train to Cirencester, weekend at the cottage.

And Elie says, Your writing is so good, it will happen soon, really – try another agent. He picks his tooth with a toothpick.

Oh thanks, Elie, I think – with your second detective novel, one academic book, publishing job, wife from L'École Normale Supérieure, Paris flat, Dordogne house. Yes, thank you, Elie Robert-Nicoud, Monsieur Establishment.

My god, I feel fantastic when I stand up, whoops! fantastic. I have a strong hard piss, like a fireman's hose on full pressure. I sidle up to the bar to pay the bill. Do I have enough cash? How much! My face remains like stone and on the back of the bill I write, Let's go out: phone number? She does! She does!

Elie jumps in a cab. Goodbye! Goodbye Elie!

I walk up Queen Victoria Street.

The good oysters burble inside me and the sea-soul taste returns. Thank you thank you life is weird life is great. I am a big plump oyster with a gorgeous mollusc's phone number itching like a pearl under my shell.

Stolen Dreams
1970s

Tal-y-bont Dreams

Rolling down from Snowdon, the winter storm had gathered all day. I was spending the night at John's cottage, up a lane going east from Tal-y-bont towards Bedd Taliesin. Having split up with my girlfriend I was going back to mid 1970s London tomorrow.

'It was never going to work,' John said.

'S'pose not.'

John stoked the fire and jumped back into his brass bed. I slugged the cider in the other bed and passed him the bottle. I put my train ticket on the mantelpiece.

'Like being in the army.' He pulled on the joint.

There was no heating downstairs.

'What are you reading?' he asked.

'I'm reading about Taliesin, from *The Mabinogion*.'

'Who's that?'

I snuggled into my bed and held up the book: 'I Taliesin, chief of bards/With a sapient Druid's words...'

'Do you want to hear John Martyn?'

'It was worth being a bard,' I said, 'they invoked celestial power and their poems united the tribe round their leader.'

Wind spun over the hills. If you followed the track past the farm, you came to a remnant of a bronze-age cairn where Taliesin was supposed to be buried. Three months ago, before things went wrong, I sat on it and overlooked the estuary and the blue diamond sea.

'I'm going to Spain in the spring,' John said.

'Why are you so happy, didn't you want the commune to work?'

'Of course I did, but cling to nothing, man. That's the way.'

Wind hummed and raindrops were loud on the window.

'And then I Taliesin/Chief of the bards of the west.'

'I want to listen to the music.' John turned off the light.

Hot ashes spat in the wood fire. The flames shaped images of those I had known during my nine months in Wales, of the things we had done, the places I had seen.

John pulled the covers over his head. I turned on the torch and read the first page of the Taliesin story: 'For it was the beginning of Arthur's time and of the Round Table.' Taliesin had been found as a boy floating in a coracle on a river near here. As a man he had travelled all over Wales, and known incarnations in other times. When I sat by his burial place, his presence spoke in the trees, in the smell of peat and wind, of soil and grass.

'Night, John.'

My London train ticket was crisscrossed by shadows from the fire.

Hornsey Rise

In 1975 Hornsey Rise was reputed to be the largest squat in Europe. The 14 bus dropped me at the bottom of the hill. From out of the warm July air garlic and kebab smells made me feel hungry.

Along the rise were three large Greater London Council blocks of flats: Welby House, Goldie House, Richie House. A barbed wire perimeter fence erected by the council had been torn down. Strips of colourful material hung along its length, as if Red Indians had mounted a successful raid on a cowboy encampment.

The entrance to Welby House was blocked by bags of old clothes, rubbish, abandoned cars, broken fridges and cookers. Banners flapped loosely over the railings on the third and fourth floors:

'Don't Dump Rubbish!'

'Order your organic vegetables from flat 221.'

'Meeting about the future tomorrow in the square.'

'Stay Cosmic, Meditate.'

'Hornsey Rising Yippee!'

Whiffs of urine spiced the air as I knocked on 286 Welby House, my contact address. Crudely nailed-on planks of wood indicated that no one was living there. A man came out from the flat next door and asked me what I wanted. Tall with straggly-fair hair, multi-coloured beads dangled round his tanned neck, and a white tie-dyed T-shirt made him look like a beach bum lost in the city. I explained that I needed somewhere to live. 'I'm Graham,' he said with a big open smile. He made me feel that my hippy dreams could still come true.

In his large living room, tarot cards were spread on the floor, a pretty girl looked up from them and said 'Hello' softly in a French accent. She held 'The Star' in

29

her hand. I smiled too enthusiastically. The towel was kissing the smooth skin above her breasts; her light-brown hair cascaded in corkscrews round her elfin face. She rearranged the tarot cards and then bundled them up in a beautiful, old and faded paisley silk scarf.

Graham's Lancashire accent comforted me because it reminded me of my mother's pride in her Lancashire roots, and I felt at home, as if a distant family member was making me welcome. A large bunch of keys jangled in his hand and he explained that he was the local estate agent and that 'it was time we saw a few properties'.

Half an hour later, having handed over five pounds, I looked out from the window of my one-bedroom flat, five doors away from Eloise and Graham's place. A little girl was making daisy chains in the rubbish-strewn square.

I laid out my sleeping bag and unpacked my rucksack. I placed on the floor the brass rubbing of the Celtic Cross I had bought in Galway. It wasn't a God thing, but a spiritual sense that all the separate parts connected in wholeness – the kind of revolution I wanted. I tucked the Krishnamurti book under my sleeping bag. Through the open window came the sounds of one of my favourite groups, America – and this was a good omen.

Later in the week I went to a 'Hornsey Rising' meeting and joined a discussion group, 'Alternative Visions'. On the Friday of the second week Graham and Eloise invited me for a meal. As I walked in, Irish Paul, who I got to know in the months ahead, handed me a joint. A few other people were mingling around. Half-an-hour later Eloise carried in an earthenware pot with a pointy bottom. We sat in a circle on the floor. The aromatic steam from the rich sauce floated round us. As I closed my eyes an atmosphere of freedom embraced me. This promised a different world from the Home Counties of my family life. Eloise put a blob of couscous on each plate. The savoury sauce was different from anything I had eaten before. Candlelight flickered on the pot.

I asked the Italian man sitting next to me what he was doing in London. 'Resting out for a while.' He smiled. His bearded Italian friend gave him a cautionary glance. Eloise's hand touched my shoulder as she passed the wine.

When we had finished eating, Graham told stories about when he was a railway worker in Blackburn and how they had stolen 'a load of railway sleepers and made a fucking brilliant little hut where we smoked dope all day'. A cross-eyed anarchist, Johnno, with a large, balding head and a cut-glass accent talked about 'the gr-e-a-a-a-t challenge of forming collectives'. Ian, a thin, sour-faced Scot, a secondary-school teacher and People's Revolutionary Party activist, told the anarchist he was 'being simplistic'. Bella, a freaky psychiatric nurse, was training to be a Laingian therapist. Irish Paul stripped lead off roofs whenever he could find the work. Charlie, about eighteen, skinny and pockmarked, had the saddest brown eyes I had ever seen. He was the only person younger than me and he hardly said a word.

After dinner we shared a hookah and drank mint tea. Ian's voice rose to a higher-pitched whine as he quarrelled about 'the inadequacy of Johnno's overview and the inevitability of a real Marxist workers' revolution'. Johnno laughed and Ian grew angrier. I could imagine Ian, after the revolution, as a witch-hunter general, chairing a committee that interrogated all those whose views he considered deviant, and shooting them, or perhaps offering retraining at a 'Correction Centre'.

From the kitchen, Graham and Eloise's jollity made me feel isolated. Bella moved next to me, sat cross-legged and rocked slightly. 'You got a girlfriend?' she asked. I smiled into her dark eyes and said 'not at the moment.' She asked if I was 'engaged with feminist issues'.

'What do you mean by 'engaged?' I replied coolly.

'Can't men ever answer a straight question?' She almost spat at me.

I edged away. Ian and Johnno were shouting. Irish Paul was sitting on the window ledge and came into the centre of the room. 'I tink you're all a bunch of middle-class tossers!' He tapped me on the shoulder and led me to the corner. 'Take no notice, she's a lezzie, dat's her ting. She wants to cut off all our willies.'

Charlie, the lonely boy, was scraping his fingers down the window. Irish Paul drew me aside again. 'He's doing well,' he whispered, 'off heroin for three weeks now.'

Glass smashed in the square. We huddled round the window. A motorbike gang with 'Hells Demons' sewn into the back of their black leather jackets, roamed like a pack of wolves. They stood outside a ground floor flat and then knocked in the door with a sledgehammer. They dragged out a small, terrified man.

Eloise rushed in. 'They came back!'

'Come on,' Graham said, 'let's go and stop them.'

No one responded. Other people stared from flats in the square. No one said anything.

'Surely we can help?' I said to Paul.

'No, no, I don't think so, they'll go soon.'

The flat smelt stale of old carpets and lack of cleaning. Outside, a half-full Newcastle-brown bottle spun for twenty yards, then hissed and cracked against a tree.

The Hells Demons encircled the man and kicked him to the floor. After a while they lost interest and the man writhed, blood trickling from his nose.

'Don't you think,' I eyeballed Ian, 'that it would have been worth stopping them?'

'That would have been a very adolescent response,' he said, turning away.

Stolen Dreams

The track became single-line after Shrewsbury as the train began its steady climb over the border country between England and Wales. 'Come and see us soon.' I read Eloise's letter again, then stuffed it in my back pocket. Near Machynlleth, herons were nesting high above the river that led to the estuary.

It was good to be out of London. In the autumn of 1975 the council had threatened a mass eviction of the squats in Hornsey Rise, and it was like living amongst a pack of wolves. Most of the good people had left. Graham and Eloise had moved out to Wales.

At Aberystwyth the branch line took me north towards Pwllheli and I got off at a small deserted station where no one collected tickets and the seagulls squawked. A very old couple, the woman in a Paisley shawl and the man with a cloth cap, hobbled on to a train. As it pulled away from the platform, the old couple's wrinkled, smiling faces looked at me.

'2 Rhyadrid Road, above the tobacconist'. I came to an area like an old port, with disused railway-tracks sunk in cracked concrete, where the shunters would once have pushed the slate towards the waiting tramp ships. Beyond that was a solitary terrace. The tobacconist's shop was on the corner.

Eloise opened the front door and hugged me. 'Université, comme-et-il?' she asked, and led me up the narrow stairs. I hoped that Graham was not there. At the other side of the door, which was inset with thick rectangular panes of frosted-glass, Graham was sprawled out on a chintzy-red sofa. 'Long bloody way from Hornsey, eh?' He grinned at me.

The sea pattered outside. Eloise made coffee in the kitchen, her lips pouting. Her body was taut and thin through her dress. As she stood by me her breasts rubbed against my shoulder. She skipped across the floor as she searched in the cupboards for the brown sugar. I wanted her to look at me, to remember how well we got on in Hornsey, of that time when Graham was away and she came back to my flat after a party and slipped into my bed. She said, 'No, it's my period, but maybe another time? Graham doesn't believe in "commitment" so why should I?' I slept with my arms round her. Perhaps Graham guessed something?

The primitive coffee percolator burbled on the stove.

'Keep still!' I said.

She tried to dash past but I held her wrists.

'Not everything is great,' she whispered. Her eyes were red from crying. 'Do you still see that snobby girlfriend?'

'We must talk,' I said.

'Maybe. Coffee?'

We sat in the main room with Graham and smoked one of his special, torpedo-shaped joints. 'We're going to give you a good time, Simon, it's great to see you,' he said.

Sprawling out on the comfy sofa, the calm of the not-London scene eased my body. 'It's nice to be here,' I said. For a while the tick of the clock seemed to be the only movement in the room.

'Who's that?' Eloise jumped to her feet at the sound of three knocks on the door. She tried to blow away the smoke, Graham rushed to open the window. Eloise took a deep breath and walked serenely down the stairs. 'Mr Edwards, what a surprise.'

Graham pretended to hide behind the sofa. Eloise ran up, fumbled under cushions, retrieved bits of money. Graham turned his pockets inside out. 'Are you there?' a Welsh voice called up. I handed Eloise a five-pound-note, her quick kiss tickled my nose. Downstairs she asked, 'How is your wife?' and he said that Mrs Edwards was still suffering from her back. 'I'm sorry,' Eloise responded, 'have they caught the thieves yet?' He said they had not. Mr Edwards owned the tobacconist's shop beneath their flat.

That evening we went for a walk. The slate tiles of the terrace glistened beneath watery moonlight. At the side of the quay a stacked pile of railway sleepers were rotting. 'This would have been a real busy little place once,' Graham said. Behind us a hill of slate was slowly collapsing towards the sea.

He pointed to the little port and said it would be the perfect place for an organic food stall, 'You could encourage the communes in Wales to join in.' He dug his hands into his pockets and scanned the horizon as if he was hoping to see a load of Welsh hippies coming over the hills. He walked off, kicking the gravel.

Back at their place we had a meal, drank a lot of cider, and played cards. From the top of the Welsh dresser Graham brought down a box, on the front of which was a picture of bearded Edwardian men in dinner suits, puffing their cigars in subdued ecstasy. He handed me a big cigar, and squeezed one between his lips. 'Bloody great that bastard Nixon resigned in the end,' he said. He looked as content as any corrupt capitalist as the smoke plumed from the tip of his cigar.

From behind the sofa he drew out different packets of cigars and cigarettes, as well as several loose King Edward the V11 Coronas. Pulling out two large suitcases from under the sofa, he flicked open the lids to reveal a treasure chest of tobacco products.

'It was you, wasn't it? You ripped off the tobacconist!'

Graham's shoulders hunched and he ran his fingers through his hair. 'Please take them back to London, sell them, I've been bloody stupid…'

'Did you ask me down just for that?' I stubbed out my cigar and went out.

When I returned twenty minutes later no more was said about the request. We stuffed the merchandise back into the cases. Graham went to have a bath.

Drizzle clouds gathered over the sea. I opened the window and a spray of rain refreshed my face. When I scanned the seashore there were no lights to be seen.

'You okay?' Eloise stroked my back. I shook her away. Then she put both hands on my shoulder, I turned, and her breath tasted sweet on my tongue. She touched my cheek, then kissed me.

When the bath water began to gurgle we disentangled ourselves.

Eloise made tea, and we relaxed to John Martyn's *Bless the Weather*. A loud knock on the door startled us.

Graham ran down and we listened from the top of the stairs.

'I'm detective-constable Brooks. I happened to be passing. Thank you for reporting the robbery at the tobacconists. It must have scared you.'

'Yeah. Worse than London! Couldn't believe it. Have you caught them yet?'

'We don't know it's "them", but we are following certain leads.' He coughed. 'Am I right that you're out of work?'

Graham mumbled. They talked in hushed voices for a few minutes.

'I'll get in touch if I need to. Goodnight.'

Graham came up, ashen faced. We sat around glumly and watched television. They went to bed about 1pm.

Soon Graham began to snore. I made up a bed of cushions on the floor and piled old blankets over me. Draughts, and sounds from outside, found a way through my woollen igloo.

I heard footsteps. I sat up.

'Please take one suitcase of cigarettes. Graham has been so stupid,' she whispered.

'No,' I said coldly. She kissed me slowly and undid her Chinese silk dressing gown. 'No,' I said, 'No.'

The next morning Graham slept late. Eloise put a mug of real coffee beside me and the aroma blew away my bad thoughts. Sharp light burst through the chink in the curtains.

'Can you spare a cigarette?' I asked Eloise and we giggled. I had a second coffee. 'I'll take some stuff back to London.'

She sat beside me and glanced at the bookshelf.

'Are you still reading them?' I asked.

'All the time.'

There was a pack of tarot cards on the bottom shelf, an old French set created by Jean Noblet, which had belonged to her grandmother in Marseilles.

When we first met last year she did a reading for me, and laid out the cards in a pattern. 'The Hanged Man' had come up in a significant position. 'Don't worry,' she reassured me, 'it is about change, that is all, about something dying so a new thing can live. And look where you have "The Star" – fantastique!'

Later, we walked up the slate hill and the sea looked green. It was Sunday and the pubs were shut, so we had a picnic of beer and sandwiches. The rest of the day passed in a happy haze.

The next morning Eloise waved me off on the platform. Travelling towards London, the cottages and houses seemed full of secrets.

My squat had not been broken into and the shiny packages of cigarettes and cigars cheered up the living room. I organised them in piles and worked out how much money I could make.

At first I sold cigarettes to people I knew, then I became more daring and sold them from the corner of the student-union bar. Within two weeks over half of them had gone. I hid the money under the floorboards.

One Friday evening a loud knock at the door startled me and I checked that all my illicit goods were packed away. Eloise stood there like a waif.

'Graham is making me crazy,' she said.

Sitting by the window she was shocked by how broken down all the flats round the square looked. 'The dream is over, don't you know that?' she said.

I kissed her. We went out for an Indian meal, and when we returned Eloise took a bath. The hot gushing taps opened dreams of the future.

She came in wearing her Chinese gown, which glowed like a magic lamp. She turned off the main light, we shared a joint, and she eased herself over me. There was no rush. My dream was nowhere else but here. Her skin was silkier than her gown.

She asked me afterwards why I wanted to live in all this deadness. 'Listen,' she said, 'listen.' And she didn't sound like a child as she talked about ways we could make money. How much happier I would be if I changed, and I would look even more gorgeous in a good suit.

Lou Reed's *Transformer* was playing from one of the flats and Eloise sang the words. I could almost taste the money I had stashed under the floorboards.

So we settled down together and at first everything was perfect. Eloise had brought another case of cigarettes from Wales, and we sold them round the squats.

One morning we went into the West End and bought me a lovely, dark pinstriped suit, a shirt and a tie, from Herbie Frogg. The next day we drank wine in the French Pub in Soho and had lunch at the Gay Hussar. It felt like Bonnie and Clyde. Over pudding she talked about her contact in Notting Hill, 'an older woman, French, very professional. She deals in cheque-books.' On the bus home, her profile made me think of a seductive witch. Then we made love again and I didn't care what she did so long as she stayed.

Over the next two months she sometimes dressed up smartly and went off on her own for the day, and never said why. One night I asked her where she had been, her lips turned tight and her eyebrows rose. She glared like I was a child.

'What's going on?' I shouted and she said quietly, 'Don't ask, Simon, it's much better.' I pulled off her shoulder bag and dug my hand inside. My shin recoiled from her vicious kick, I pushed her, she fell over. The contents of her bag tipped out. I picked out two cheque-books, neither of which belonged to Eloise, someone else's cheque card, and an American Express card. 'No,' I said, 'no more.' I saw the police detective from Wales standing on our doorstep: 'We have reason to think you can help us with our enquiries.' I didn't want to become a real criminal.

One night I reached out for her in my sleep but she was not there. A week later she wrote to say she had moved back to Marseilles and she would never forget me. She gave an address but never replied to the several letters I sent. Under the bed she had put the tarot cards, wrapped in her silk Chinese gown.

Punk Music Blues

I always worried that my squat may have been burgled while I was out. That particular night, a February Friday in 1976, I felt especially insecure. Last week someone had tried to break in, but the heavy padlock on the front door had deterred them. The frame had been damaged where someone had attempted to dig out the back plate of the padlock.

I felt edgy as I set off. I was meeting a friend who was a convert to punk music. I hated everything about punk. The icy-cold wind had disinfected the tenement corridors and taken away the smell of urine. An aroma of soil and root crops wafted out of my minivan as I opened the door – I used to collect the organic vegetables for our community stores – and the smell hung around. As I drove down Highgate Hill, London glowed.

The Rochester Castle was a pub in Stoke Newington and a centre for punk music. Most nights, repulsive bands would clamber on to the stage and vomit out their noise.

I called 'Hello' to my friend Bertie who was ensconced with a group of punks at a table in the far corner: two of the boys wore black greasy-and-torn leather jackets decorated with safety pins. Their Domestos-bleached, kitchen-scissors-cut hair was gelled into stiffness; the girls had white death-mask make-up on their faces and their eyes were smeared with black mascara. Everyone looked angry.

As I walked through the pub, keeping an eye on the floor for spit and chewing gum, I bumped into a big punk. Dangling chains round his neck sparkled. There were open safety pins in his jacket and I touched the silver ankh I wore beneath my shirt – and then felt stupid – as if that would make any difference.

40

'Simon, over here!' Bertie said cheerily, his vicary voice rising above the hubbub. His long fair hair and cherubic face made him look like an alternative-culture boy scout.

Bertie owned a very small recording studio. He had made a name for himself by promoting punk bands, and had carved out a niche in this market. I never wanted to ask if he really liked their music because I should have been depressed if the answer was yes. The band tonight was a new one, the Sex Pests, and he said they were 'truly original'.

Punks huddled together like Gothic gravediggers. Two very tall ones, in full punk uniform, zombied up to the bar and stamped their fists. They made grunty, guttural sounds as if English was a recent experience.

'Won't be a minute,' Bertie said and spoke to the boys at the bar.

They came back with Bertie to our table. I didn't want to know these death wishers: 'I'm Fred Vile,' he said, looking skeletal. He gobbed on the floor. The other one grabbed my hand in his long bony fingers. 'I'm fuckin' Johnnie Dead.' His dark eyes sucked me towards a black hole.

'I'm Simon.'

Johnnie pulled my hand until it was pressed against his ribcage.

'All right, Johnnie, all right,' Bertie the punk-handler said, 'Simon's an old friend. Save all that for the stage.'

Johnnie let go and snarled. I hated their posey violence more than I hated the straight world. He shouldn't have been attacking me. But who was the enemy now? Bertie was unperturbed by the incident. Soon after this the two punks jumped on to the stage, and a couple of others joined them. Their out-of-tune instruments made long, distorted notes.

On the yellowed ceiling two globes studded with mirror glass sent rainbow lights into my mind.

'Incredible, don't you think?' Bertie nudged me in the ribs.

I closed my eyes but my mind was filled with an image of four jackbooted punks marching on my dreams…. I opened my eyes. Punks began to pogo-dance, their arms clasped to their sides to increase projection, their heads rolling.

I stood in the corner, pulled my long hair and scratched my flowery shirt. Bertie was chatting to people at the other side of the pub. The Sex Pests played an encore, which sounded exactly the same as the crap they had been playing all evening.

Finally, the music stopped. I sat again with Bertie, who praised the noise, and called it 'the most exciting thing that had happened since The Velvet Underground – we're in Punkland!'

Punkland, I thought, *I'd rather be in Disneyland.*

Johnnie and Fred came over, and stubbed out their cigarettes under their crudely decorated black boots.

Johnnie Dead whispered something to Bertie, who then turned to me, 'There's a party later, keep it quiet, you've been invited too…Got to chat with Fred….'

Johnnie clunked up to me, 'Wanna meet a couple of me mates?'

In the middle of the pub a group of his friends were sprawled over seats, 'Ere's an old hippy mate of mine, mannnnn.'

Two women punks sat nearby, turned heavy rings on their fingers. I told them about my recent trip to Wales. They asked if I had found a lot of magic mushrooms, then cackled. The others continued to talk loudly all round me.

After what seemed a long time Johnnie grabbed me by the shoulder, 'Time for the fucking party.' Lesser punks scattered as this noble personage led the way out. On the pavement he tugged my arm, S'pose you think we're a load of thick bastards?'

'I think you did really well to get your band together.'

'What do you fuckin' know?'

'As much as you, that's for sure.'

We punk-marched down Stoke Newington High Street. I kept a step behind him because his arms and legs were as anarchic and disorderly as his music. The back of his leather jacket was tooled with black and chrome studs.

'Ugly 'ole innit?' he said when we reached Abney Park cemetery.

I couldn't think straight or swallow.

'I won't come to the party, thanks Johnnie.'

'What? Don't think we share your "visionnnn", shit 'ead – dope and daisy chains, university people talking about Sartr-er and Nietzsch-er. You're all dead, mate.'

'So what's your vision?'

'My vision is razorblades.'

'Bye, Johnnie.'

We walked off in opposite directions.

Lord Carbuncle's Dancing Hours

My life was poised between nothings in the London of the late 1970s as I hovered round the edge of other people's worlds. The city was in a state of alert for IRA bombs. It was a shock to see armed policemen patrolling the streets of the West End, guarding key installations in many other places, and setting up roadblocks.

A good friend, Harry, lived in an enormous squat in Carburton Street, with a number of other people I didn't especially like. They called the house 'Carbuncle' and the name was displayed in bold Gothic lettering on their front door.

Boy George, not yet the famous pop star, lived round the corner in Great Titchfield Street with a bunch of weirdos. They came alive at night, like Draculas rising from the dead, and went clubbing. They moved on after a few years.

Carburton Street, a rundown but elegant Georgian terrace, was under threat of demolition. Even the attempts of John Betjeman could not save it. The terrace was demolished in 1980, along with others, to make way for an ugly hotel. The ghosts of Carburton Street live on.

I spent some of my week in the Bayswater flat of an eccentric barrister for whom I worked part-time as a chauffeur and general assistant. One morning in November I woke on the sofa bed in the large sitting room. Trees in the square were bare against the grey sky.

Downstairs the postman had delivered a large envelope for me:

Carbuncle
22 Carburton St
London W2
Tel: 01 388 5427

Official Declaration

Simon Carver
Is invited to
Lord Carbuncle's Ball
on the occasion of the coming out
of his daughter
Lady Cecilia
To be celebrated on the
Ninth day of December, 1978
at *Carbuncle*

Formal Dress:
Black Ties Long Dresses Tiaras Spats Top Hats Cummerbunds War Medals
Strictly no Bounders Hoi Poloi Commoners or Cads
Foreign Diplomats may wear indigenous attire if necessary for religious observance

It was a striking invitation but it did not fill me with joy. Carbuncle's walls were damp; the height of the rooms, rather than lift the spirits, seemed to trap you in a malign castle. The kitchen was squalid, the basement oppressive.

A week later I set off. I was going to help them get things together.

The brickwork along the Carburton street terrace was darkened from decades of London soot. Chimney pots were crooked, window frames rotten. On the Post Office Tower, which looked like a spaceship, lights blip-blipped round the perimeter at the top. Everyone knew MI5 had installed listening equipment to enable them to tap into phone lines in Britain, Ireland and Europe.

I rattled the cast-iron knocker of the large lime-green door. Harry opened it. He was tall and good-looking with dreamy poet's eyes. He rubbed glue from his trousers and with his other hand devoured late-breakfast toast. I followed him to his room in the basement.

Next to the fireplace was a 'SlopeRider', an invention of Harry's, on which you sat in order to whiz down hills at speed. He hoped it would make him lots of money and he had applied for a patent. This contraption, and his lively sex life with a variety of attractive young women, sustained his spirits.

Harry's was the largest room, more workshop than bedroom; square and hung with curtains that hid dark walls. Wind whistled down the chimney of the range.

'How are things going?' I propped myself against his workbench.

'Pretty stormy.'

He worked his paintbrush along the sides of the fibre-glass SlopeRider.

I sat down in the broken leather armchair by the wall. A strand of crumbling wallpaper peeled off as I touched it. I rubbed off more layers until I reached the dark mahogany-coloured oil paint, which must have been the original coat. The plaster granulated into dust.

Harry showed me the clothes he was wearing for the party: an Oxfam dinner jacket in good condition; a purple cummerbund; a row of medals. I was getting excited about the party, from an energy of desperation, like 'Tigers, tigers burning bright', against the encroaching fascist night. (Conspiracy theories haunted us. We were sure that Thatcher had a deal with Securicor to use their vehicles in the event of civil disturbance.)

Harry's gluey paintbrush rested in a jar of Gunk. From under the bed he pulled out a chipped dark-wood tuck box. He opened it and took out a letter he had found last month when applying Cuprinol to the joists.

He handed it to me. It was written by someone called John Flaxman on very old yellowed paper:

17th May, 1809
7, Great Titchfield Street

My Dear Joseph

Your amiable dinner last night was a great delight to me.

I much enjoyed the company at your table of dear William Blake, that grand cultivator of the Pure Pleasures — drinking and jolly chatter — and not I fear the Pure Pleasures of which Mr Wordsworth would approve! Blake's scurrilous remarks about the 'Lakers' were invigorating. But I have to dissent, and fear I was not candid enough last evening, about his ungenerous remarks concerning Josiah Wedgwood.

I surely could not have done better than employ my small abilities in the service of so worthy a patron as Wedgwood, who was so kind as to send me to Rome, the very fountainhead of taste in the fine arts. I was delighted in return to be able to employ my industry as a designer for him.

Having spent many days and months in the study of classical sculpture, I designed the frieze of what Wedgwood has generously called one of his most popular pieces, 'The Dancing Hours', a celebration of the marriage of Cupid, depicting women dancing in a circle. I sent the frieze off to his factory at Etruria in 1788, and Wedgwood had just perfected the tinted blue glazing of the fine jasper porcelain, which I believe is already being described as 'Wedgwood Blue'.

It is not calamitous news to my ears, as the over enthusiastic Blake suggested last evening, that Wedgwood has profited financially by my design. Indeed, I am delighted he has done so!

Your affectionate friend,
John Flaxman

'Harry, it's amazing! Who was John Flaxman?'

Harry said that he was a Neo-Classical sculptor who had made enormous, complicated funeral sculptures for

Westminster Abbey and Chichester Cathedral. He died in 1826. A furniture maker, Joseph Groves, lived in this house – and was a friend of Flaxman, who lived nearby and must have come here for dinner. I forgot the ugliness around me: I saw wooden surfaces polished with beeswax, paintwork restored to brightness, the house glowing with candlelight. I found a rough bit on Harry's SlopeRider. 'Give me some sandpaper, I'll smooth it off.'

'Do you think my craftsmanship is crap then?' He kicked a shoe across the room.

'Hey, Harry, it's fine.'

'This is the 1970s. Who cares about spending a hundred years on French polishing a piece of wood.' He banged his fist against the wall and behind it loose pieces fell in the hollow of the lathe-and-plaster. 'People want fun. I can't stand this place anymore.'

'It'll be great. Don't worry.'

'If this project fails, I don't know what I'll do.'

He put his head in his hands and sat on the bed.

We went upstairs to the double sitting room, pulled back the dividing shutters to make one large space, and moved furniture in preparation for the party. Was this where Joseph Groves had entertained John Flaxman?

At the local café we ate thick bacon sandwiches and drank mugs of strong instant coffee. A 'Bomb Warning' poster behind the counter told us to be alert for strange packages as the IRA were having a surge to blow up London before Christmas. A red anti-terrorist police car raced up the road.

We gossiped about friends and girls, but I wanted to know about John Flaxman and Joseph Groves. Harry was well informed and said that Groves often made things in this house. I imagined him shaping a chair, or dowelling the legs. He had been a well-known furniture maker and worked for Chippendales before setting up with Mr Heal in Tottenham Court Road. Flaxman had a studio in Soho Square. Their lives felt solid and real.

That evening we drank in The Spread Eagle, off Regent's Park Road. Policemen patrolled the pavements. A sniffer dog yelped at me. The dog-handler called 'Oih, you lads, come over here.' His partner asked us who we were and where we were going. We showed him our driving licences. His walkie-talkie crackled as he spoke to a colleague. Then he let us go.

I slept in the dingy basement 'guest room', listening to noises from the pavement. In an *A to Z* I followed the route John Flaxman would have taken to work in those slow-time days: sauntering from Great Titchfield Street to Wedgwood's workshop, through Wells Street, Berwick Street, and then Carlisle Street and into Soho Square.

Police sirens screamed up the road as if they were coming to this house.

In the late morning we started preparing for the party. I cut up cucumbers and oranges. At least 80 people were expected.

Some guests, those staying the night, arrived about six. People got togged up in every available space. A bomb had gone off near Brixton and the Northern Line was out of action. The Doors 'Waiting for the Sun' blasted out of the stereo. 'Get up to date, you sad old hippies!' someone said.

The evening swept on in a haze of drink and dope. We discussed our plans for the summer, desperate to stay ahead of the collapsing world. There were many 'Hellos', 'Good to see you', 'Been so long.'

A three-tiered cake was carried in by a girl dressed as Cleopatra and announced by a trumpeter. Freddy, who lived in the house, and was training to be a chartered accountant, looked ravishing as Lady Cecilia. He left a red kiss on my cheek.

Happy guests filled the house, sitting on the stairs, crowding the rooms. I was wearing a gold kaftan and top hat. Miles had come in an alligator suit; Matilde was wearing a white sari. Alan had secretly borrowed his father's Royal Navy commander's uniform, Abigail came as Oliver Twist. Others had painted faces. We mingled and became part of a strange tribe.

I stood by the window. Policemen were bundled up in flak jackets and blue police Transit vans roamed the streets with lights flashing. Armed policemen huddled at their stations round the Post Office Tower. There seemed to be rumours of bombs on every corner.

Satin material covered the lights in the sitting room. The cannabis had made me hallucinatory and I was floating. I clasped revellers by their arms and swirled them round. Harry, perfectly dressed as Lord Carbuncle, was uniting the party with tales of shooting tigers out in India. Waves of people danced and the wide oak floorboards heaved gently.

Lord Carbuncle cast aside all cares and twirled a dark-haired beauty across the room. From a crack in the wall I saw Flaxman lead a procession of Carbuncle ghosts, here to dance for the last time.

Snow began to fall. The tips of the policemen's helmets had turned white.

The Copper Tank

'There's plenty squats in Stoke Newington, don't worry yourself,' Irish Paul said.

By the late-1970s it had become difficult to find good squats in Hackney. The council were vandalizing their own properties – smashing up lavatories and sinks, pulling out gas and electricity metres – in order to deter squatters.

I helped Paul carry the water tank into his living room where it joined the other five on the floor.

'Good money in those,' Paul said, 'and there's one for you.'

'Keep them, it's okay.'

I stared at it: coppery tones, about four feet high, bulbous, a foot in width, with the top and bottom compressed into the collar shape of a wine flagon.

'Take it, and more than that, I'm off to Stoke Newington now on business, I can show you a few properties.'

With a spotty gipsy scarf he wiped the sweat from his forehead, shook his bushy dark hair and walked out. I picked up the tank, which was surprisingly light, followed Paul to his battered green Transit, and laid it in the back. We set off.

At the beginning of Stoke Newington the street curved like a country lane. The railings of an old Georgian house sparkled under the sheen of rain. The Elizabethan church was set back snugly from the main road. The tank crashed against the back door of the van, and I slipped over my seat to put my arms round it.

The van jerked to a halt outside The Crown and Paul got out. Behind the plate glass windows, black faces and longhaired white freaks jostled together as Bob Marley beat out from the jukebox. The neon gloss on the roads, buildings and cars projected shadows at strange angles. With a couple of old blankets I made the tank more secure. A few minutes later Paul jumped in, carrying a tightly wrapped brown parcel. He placed it carefully under the driver's seat.

We parked at the far end of Clissold Park and Paul said that his friends might be able to fix me up with somewhere to live, and take the tank off me for a few quid. I manoeuvred it out of the van.

We stood at the front door of a three-storey Victorian house. The garden was overgrown with high grass and rose bushes. Paul tugged the bell pull.

'What you want?' a short thickset man said.

'Lisa and Danny in?' Paul asked.

'Don't know.'

A pretty, willowy girl came up behind him.

'Hello, Lisa,' Paul said.

She led us through the house to the kitchen.

'Danny around?' Paul asked.

'He's gone to Archway to pick up a guitar, a Des Paul, or something.'

'This is me mate, copper water tank,' Paul quipped. 'Oh, there you are, Simon.'

It rattled as I lay it on the hallway floor.

In the kitchen the red linoleum was cracked and beneath that the stained floorboards were splintered. Lisa made us mugs of tea. Her nails were bitten down.

Paul gulped his tea, 'Got to crack on.'

'The tank!' I said.

'It'll be fine.'

'Paul…'

He rushed out.

'I'm sorry,' I said.

A single bulb shone on the patina of greasy surfaces. Lisa sipped nettle tea as she glanced at the water tank in the hallway.

'Might get stolen, you never know who's around.' She looked at me for the first time. 'Keep it my room for a few days, it'll be safe there.'

I followed her up two flights of stairs, the water tank clanging on the steps. 'That's Danny's room,' she pointed across the corridor, 'we're lucky to have two, he does a lot of practising.'

'I lay it on its side by their, her, mattress on the floor.

'That's very nice,' she said.

Richly patterned carpets had been nailed to the damp walls. There was a large, tatty Iranian rug over the bare boards and a curved-back Victorian couch in the middle of the room, its burgundy velvet fabric torn. She switched on two lamps, closed the window shutters, lit a joss stick and a paraffin heater.

'I'm really getting into art.' She rolled the tank into the middle of the floor, 'I think I'll draw that.'

The tank's yellow-red tinges were enhanced by the lamps. She pressed her hand at one end and I held mine at the other until it was still. With a cloth she buffed up the tank's top. 'Yeah, I can do something with that.'

'Do you...?' She held up a Thai stick.

I nodded.

She rolled a joint, her fingers shaking as she lit it. The rising smoke made shapes, which she punctured with her finger. She blew puffs through the inlet hole and smoke spumed out from the outlet hole in rings. Her palm moved along the length of the ridged copper tank, 'It's a lovely shape, and it's warmed up now. I'm going to apply to art college soon, she said. 'What do you do?'

'I had a poem in a magazine last month.'

We chatted about art and writing.

'Where did you come from, before London?' I asked.

'It's where we're going to that matters.'

'I know some really good people who are setting up a commune near Aberystwyth.'

'You at university?'

'I might drop out.'

The front door banged open.

'Don't look so guilty, Danny won't think we've been doing it.' She held the tank upright and it swayed between us. Multi-coloured glass beads glinted round her neck.

'You there?' a growly London voice called up the stairs.

'Sure, Danny.' Her facial muscles were jerky. 'I want to do a lot of sketches of it.'

'I'll drop round next week?'

'Yes.'

Danny and I shared a joke about Irish Paul, although his eyes never smiled.

During the next week I found a place to stay with a friend. On the following wet Monday morning I rang the bell of Lisa's house.

'What do you want?' the thickset man said.

'Lisa in? I've come to collect my copper tank.'

'No.'

'Can you check?'

'No.'

A throaty laugh came from upstairs. 'That's Irish Paul,' I said and sidestepped past the man.

'Be quick with that,' Paul said sharply from inside Lisa's room.

She was stuffing a wad of bank notes into a box.

'Lisa sometimes looks after cash for me,' he said, 'I knows we can trust you.'

'Of course.'

She put the shoebox under her bed, and then beneath a floorboard, which had a section cut out of it. She stood up and smiled loosely, her fingers making circles in the air.

'It's only Tuinol,' Paul said to me, 'it calms her when she gets stressed out.'

'What's that?'

'It's a downer, man, where you been.'

'I noticed spots of blood on her arm.'

'I'm not a bloody junkie!' she shouted.

'That's enough, Lisa,' Paul said. 'Go and check outside, will you.' His usually happy eyes stared coldly.

'What's this about, Paul?' I asked.

'It's nothing,' he flipped into jovial mood, 'but if you must know, I trod on the heals of a big time drug dealer, and I'm getting out, there's a Dublin rock band I'm going to manage. I'm set up now with the stash I made.'

Lisa returned and said that the car that had been outside with a man watching the house had gone.

'Bye,' Paul said.

Lisa hummed a tune from The Moody Blues *Every Good Boy Deserves Favour* and went to make chamomile tea. When she came back she closed the shutters and lit the paraffin heater.

'I'm going to change, you'll see.' She squeezed my hand. 'Look what I've done.'

The tank was in the corner now, lying along the floor, with a sidelight at either end.

'Look inside.'

I peered through a hole.

'Be careful,' she said.

An electric lead was connected to a bulb, which showed up two small clay figures, a man and a woman, painted in rainbow stripes and sitting at a small table made out of an egg box. She had managed to write a slogan above the heads of her models, 'Make Love Not War'.

'I like working in miniature.' She shook the tank but the little people and the table stayed in place.

'It's great,' I said.

'You can make some people to go in there if you want.'

'They could live in there forever.'

We rested our backs against the tank.

She tapped it. 'It's like a goblet, a canister, a cooking pot, a store ship, a balloon, it can hold all our dreams.' She touched my arm. 'Drugs get me there, and now I know that place, I'm going to stop soon, work hard at my art.' She passed me a joint. 'What does it mean to you?'

'Not sure.' I blew smoke through the inlet hole and covered the figures in fog.

That's it, man, you're getting the idea!'

'Does Danny like your work?'

'He's into his music, yes, no, don't know.'

For the next few hours we worked together as she rigged up strong lighting, fiddled with her camera, found a film under the bed, and took shots of the models in the tank for her portfolio. As the drugs wore off, her movements became more certain.

'It suits you, having a project,' I said, 'you need a change, that's all.'

I handed her the extension lead and the space between us wasn't any more, our bodies curled round each other and we kissed. We sprang apart, laughing. At the bottom end of the tank she drew a love heart shape with a thick black felt pen, and added an arrow, put two question marks inside the heart, and giggled. We sat on the bed and talked about destiny, tarot cards and Timothy Leary.

'That's Danny.' She brushed herself down.

I put the two lights back in position on either side of the tank.

'Bye,' I touched her prick-marked arm.

56

'No,' she said, 'no, it's no problem, I'm stopping. Come and see me again?'

'Yes.'

'Watcha, mate.' The door swung open. 'Come to collect your tank?'

'Lisa is using it for her art.'

'One more week.' He turned away. 'Hello, sweetheart.' They embraced with enthusiasm.

Three days later I stood outside her house again, which looked dark and empty. I could sense Lisa there, doing her art, waiting, with that strange expectant expression.

I pulled hard on the bell pull. And again.

Danny leaned out of the bedroom window. 'What do you want?'

'I came to get the tank, see Lisa.'

He went inside. 'Here's your fucking tank.' He slammed it through the open window. I huddled by the door as the tank crashed down.

'Lisa's dead.'

'What?'

'Overdose, day after you saw her.'

'I had nothing…'

'She's dead, they're doing a post-mortem.'

'I…'

'Take it. I'm moving out today. Piss off.' The window slammed shut.

Arms, legs and heads fell out of the holes in the tank. I gathered them into my pocket, and walked off with the tank. An overflow pipe was dripping down the brickwork.

I rested the tank against the park railings under a streetlight. I peeped through the hole and the trunks of the little people's bodies were still there. 'Make Love Not War'. I banged the tank against the pavement.

Night descended in muddy layers as I walked into Clissold Park. I sat on a bench in sight of the pretty Elizabethan church. Through the bare trees a three-quarter moon tinged the copper yellow. I kicked the tank to the ground; it rolled down the incline of the path and boomed.

I stopped it, smeared mud over the love heart that Lisa had drawn and carried the tank to the back of Clissold House. I placed the inlet hole beneath a tap, which I turned on.

Repairs
1990s

Breaking

Through the heat wave of a Hackney August afternoon the small gang of adolescent boys moved up Mehetabel Road like mime artists in the thick, orange air. In the east, the sky was black and closing in. I watched the boys from the side of an upstairs window.

Five boys, of different size and race, dressed in a variety of street-cred clothes: baggy jeans, baseball caps, logo T-shirts, Nikes. They rattled and shook the parking machine opposite my house.

The smallest, with skin the colour of white bread, and as thin as a Lowry figure, stood sideways on the pavement, bent his back leg and stretched his arm backwards so that it touched the ground. Then, like a Second World War grenade thrower, he hurled the egg splat against my window. The yellow yolk mixed with the white and trickled down like phlegm.

I stood in the middle of the window. The boys laughed, and ran off.

I looked at the egg, then at the boys, and felt the inside of my head boiling black. I chased them up the heat-swell of Isabella Road and into Homerton High Street. They crossed the road, the long snake of traffic gridlocked. They eased into a huddle, made mocking gestures at me.

I charged across the road and grabbed the biggest, a black boy who had jeered the most, taller than me, round faced, big limbed.

I pulled him across the road in a headlock. I hoped to drag him to the police station.

'Let me go!'

I yanked him up the incline of Homerton High Street, which felt more like a mountain now, towards the police station. My body sweated and I felt I could drown in my sweat, or at least slide away on its greasy film, until I fell out of my skin and dissolved into nothing. I tightened my arm round his neck, the other boys following us, people in cars dipping their heads in our direction, enthralled.

'Racist!' one of the boys shouted at me, and the word spun round the damp, hot sheet of the day. The word bounced around the pavements, multiplying and jumping through the open windows of the cars. 'Racist' unsettled me, sprang at my head, gashing open my forehead, which scrambled further my sense of self. I couldn't imagine that London existed out there, the art galleries, cinemas, Soho restaurants. Only the boy struggling, the others shouting, the traffic jam hissing beneath the hot, mad sky.

I managed to drag him further up the road, but now the others were surrounding me.

'Stop that!' A tall black man with dreadlocks jumped from his car. 'Leave that boy alone!'

I let him go, my shoulders dropped and I panted as the sweat dried on me.

Now the boys gathered closer round me and two of them made jerky kick shots in my direction.

'He's a fucking racist, man!' one of them said.

The large man stood behind me, and put his big hand firmly on my shoulder.

'Slow down your mouths, boys, let the man speak.'

I gabbled about the egg, the mess.

He took the boys aside, and said to one of them, 'I know your mother, so you stop associating with these kind of boys, you hear me?'

He said to me: 'Look, it's hell all ways you look – why make it worse!' He patted me on the shoulder and jumped back in to his car. The traffic jam had dispersed and he drove into the distance.

I tried to smile at the boys but my lips were glued to my teeth and the smile stuck in an ugly rictus.

'You fucking gay, man?' the small white boy asked as I tried to unstick my smile.

'Look, no more eggs, okay...?'

'Sure,' one of them said.

They sidled up the road and when they were fifty yards away the small white boy turned and showed an egg in his hand.

Heavy pellets of rain began to fall.

Hackney Sunday

On this hot July Sunday London Fields draws up like a sponge the lives and worlds of Hackney. Picnickers, loners, lovers, a unicycle that floats along the path, dogs, druggies, children, balls, Frisbees, gays, freaks, laid-back pubbers on the balcony of Pub on the Park, an old lady in a floral dress and a flowery hat dozing under a tree as if still dreaming of VE Day. Black evangelists invite us to a big tent where miracles will happen and we shall be saved. Aroma of cannabis and barbecues, wine bottles popping, beer and cider fizzing, crisps crunching. Kebabs, burgers, jerk chicken, brown rice salads, hummus, ice cream and lollies. Every shape and every kind and every race. The sky is blue as heaven as the open-air church of Hackney sings its Sunday song.

Cricket in London Fields

'You're a whore, woman!'

Dust rises as he kicks the Red Stripe can, lager squirts out along the boundary. He storms off. A teenage black girl stares mutely at the grass. A child wriggles his toes in the dust.

'Leave my boy alone!' she says, but not until the man is out of hearing range.

It is not clear if he is father or partner.

Picnickers spread across London Fields. The artificial cricket pitch looks beleaguered as the Hackney hordes move inside the boundary. By the cricket square, a baby is sick. A skinny young Asian, spread-eagled on the grass in a soiled white shirt and a cute-boy quiff, pulls hard on a cigarette. He stands, then picks up a bat.

From the shadows cool dudes walk towards the centre, in degrees of scruffiness. The Asian kid heals his fag into the ground and jogs to the middle. The umpires shoo people from the square, knock in the stumps, position the bails. Some picnickers jeer and refuse to move. Two batsmen stride to the middle, the fielders tell jokes, some button up their shirts, a few fiddle with their trainers. The umpires realise they do not have a ball.

'This place is for everyone!' a couple of youths shout.

The chorus is joined by others. A water bomb is lobbed, just missing the umpires – 'You don't own this place, man!' The motley group moves further inside the boundary.

A few minutes later the returning umpire-with-the-ball is tripped up.

The batsman takes guard. The skinny Asian marks out his run, then bowls with a smooth action at medium pace, pitches on a good length, just outside off stump.

The ball turns, past the outstretched batsman. The keeper takes the ball neatly in both hands. The ball goes from keeper to mid-on to bowler. The fielders, having walked in, now move back in loose union. The ritual of cricket creates order. During the first over the youths go outside the boundary. Ten minutes later the first wicket falls and spectators clap. The scruffy cricketers look clean and smart now.

The angry man returns, pats the child on the head, smiles at the teenage girl, picks up his Red Stripe. The rowdy boys have sneaked away.

No, Sorry, No

No, sorry, no.

Yes, I feel bad for you and your dog but it's every corner now, and why do you sit in the damp under this railway bridge at Hackney Central where the water drips down your back?

Look, I've just got off the bus from Centre Point, and walking down Tottenham Court Road is like running the gauntlet, all the *Big Issue* sellers hustling and then they give you a sarky Have a Nice Day Mate when you don't buy. Then, Dr Barnardo's people, squads of cool-looking kids, Do You Have a Moment To Help Children in Need? I avoided three sets of them. A really cute girl from Friends of the Earth asked, Would you like to talk to me, sir? I reached Heals, and relaxed as I gazed at their luxurious patio furniture – only to be harpooned from behind by a school of Save The Whalers….

Look, I'm sorry, mate, no.

Why are you sitting in this dankness, when outside the July sunshine is so bright on everyone? Your eyes are as dark as your clothes and rug, and does your dog have some sheepdog in her?

Don't these trains above you get inside your head, don't they make you feel heavy inside, and your face is white as a corpse. If you sat in the park, in the sun for an hour.

No, sorry, no.

Look over there, under the bridge the other side, those two big black guys, one without a hand, they speak French you know, very fast, Rwanda perhaps?

Your dampness, your dankness, your straggly beard – you're more like a cave dweller. Even on this bright day there is a greasy film over your hair and skin and dirty clothes. Your eyes are a dark space…. Your dog looks so thin, and thirsty, she's panting.

How the traffic roars here, all the time, it never stop, every sort of vehicle and smell – does it never make you sick?

You've been in seven squats in two years!

There he was, quite still. Sitting like a holy fool in this world that cannot stop.

'Yes, here's five pounds. Why don't you go and sit in the sun for an hour?'

Johnnie

Each week she looks more bent. Eighty-six years old, her face made up, the powder a little thick, Johnnie hobbles past our house. She was christened 'Ethel' and 'Johnnie' was the pet name given to her by her husband. Her profile is reminiscent of a Thirties model. She was born in Hackney, round the corner from Mehetabel Road. In the war she was in charge of barrage balloons near the docks. One night for a lark, rather than secure the balloon, her team let it go. She learnt to drive in the army and used to chauffeur officers. She had a lot of fun.

She lives alone in Mehetabel Road, a sitting tenant in a terraced house. She has one son, two grandchildren and a daughter-in-law. They live in Essex and visit her occasionally. Her husband was a charming Irishman who spoke like an English stage gentleman. Eighteen years ago he died in the house and a next-door neighbour helped lay out the body in the corridor. Johnny sits at night in her spotless front room, where her knickknacks sparkle.

When she walks through the churchyard she is an old lady with a stick. But the other day one of the Polish winos smiled at her. Perhaps he recognised a shared history.

Today Johnnie is on the doorstep with a tin of Brasso and a cloth, rubbing her brass letterbox and keyhole.

Lotus Flower and Cherry Blossom

Windows rattle. A May morning in Mehetabel Road and the rain swirls the litter. A twittery laugh makes me jump.

At the other side of the road a pretty Vietnamese girl is standing under the large cherry tree. She stretches for a branch. Her boyfriend's thin arms embrace her waist. She jumps. Blossom falls on their heads, which they brush away in a dance of fingers.

'Come on Minh, come on.' She pulls on his arm and giggles.

'Wait, Nhu, wait,' he says in a breezy, singsong London voice.

A flash of sunlight illuminates the nearby English trees and bushes that seem to burst into Vietnamese life as grapefruit and banana, papaya and peach flower, orchid and water lily.

Nhu and Minh kiss. He holds her tight, she wriggles free, bends on her knees. Her arms are in half moon above her head and she rises in white jeans and top to unfold like a lotus flower.

He steps back.

A car backfires, their heads turn with a quickness of fear, strange to watch. Their people's history seems to shadow them: two million killed by the Japanese in 1945, the Vietnam war with its napalm, the communists retaking of the South, the journeys of the boat people, some of whom eventually landed up in Hackney.

They smile again and skip together down the path.

Retreat

Most mornings I stop at the inscription on a black-marble grave: 'Mary Copling, Died 7 March 1866, aged 80 years.'

I love the quiet in the churchyard of St John's, Hackney. Squirrels tunnel through the fallen leaves, of beech, London plane and horse chestnut.

Mary's husband, James Copling, who died in 1856, lies beside her. They shake to dust like salt from a saltcellar, clasped together in their shiny block of history.

My mind is adrift on change.

This Monday morning I dawdle. The world begins at the other side of the graveyard. I listen to the buses.

My eyes sweep across the square of grass, felled of the gravestones that are now stacked in neat rows against the high wall of the bus garage. I look at the church, the largest parish church in London, built in 1790. Its small-bricked structure and rendered, squat white tower are solid.

Mums and dads with kids pass me on the narrow York stone path. No one smiles.

I turn right and stay in the graveyard. There is a tomb on the corner with a brass plaque added at a later date: 'Rear Admiral Sir Francis Beaufort, hydrographer for the Royal Navy from 1829-1855'. The Portland stone casket is finely crafted.

I know many names on these tombs and graves. I often rub my hands over their lettering. These people have histories and biographies: 'The relict of Edward Sheffield of The Grove in this parish, died 1859, aged 81'. (His wife died in 1849. She was taken ill on a journey to Colchester where Edward's brother was a magistrate.) I have often imagined visiting Edward at The Grove as he grew old and frail. We sit in the dark drawing room, the thick brown velvet curtains drawn back by Jane, the young maid.

But I hear noises from now: men shouting; people babbling into mobile phones; jack hammers from a building-site.

'Susannah Taverner, died 1884, 59-years-old.' Her life was modest: a governess.

The marble column of John James Ronaldson is assertive. He had a large property, Halse Hall, in Jamaica. Was his wealth from sugar, rum and slaves?

I walk round the square. I stand by Mary Copling. Next to Mary is a small mummy-shaped coffin, popular with Victorians during that period when Egyptian culture was high fashion. I kneel down and from the end of the coffin I take out the two large bricks I had loosened last month. For a moment the graveyard footpath is free of pedestrians.

On my belly I slide in to the coffin. I had previously managed to tie garden twine round the two large bricks, and left a length of twine dangling at the side so that I could pull the bricks into position behind me.

I raise my stomach. With my hands, which are wedged under me, I pull the twine and manoeuvre the bricks. I am sealed from the world. At the other end of the coffin I uncover two small holes, which I had gouged out with a chisel last month. I watch the people stumble through the graveyard.

Order

At the bus stop, all colours, ages and races. Big, small, plain, flash, tarty, weird, mad.

Oh no, not this morning, please! Coming towards me, can of beer in one hand, aluminium stick waving in the other, his face blotchy-red, hair like a silver-grey Brillo pad.

His stick scatters a young girl and a man wearing yellow lycra shorts, and he walks right up to me, the shiny glint of his stick is tickling my ribs. He pins me against the glass side of the bus shelter.

'Spare a few pence? Can yer spare some'at, mate?'

Everyone looks at us, then backs away. I can't slip out.

Then this little old black lady in a floppy white hat steps forward. 'No! Move away, you shouldn't do that. Here, me give you some chocolate and I pray for you.'

He stamps his stick on my toe.

The little black lady touches his shoulder, and turns her head to glance up the slope of Mare Street. An old white woman, with peroxide-blonde hair and face held together with foundation, looks at him too. Soon the entire straggle of us is peering up Mare Street, though I can only peer out between the little old black lady's white hat and the cropped hair of my captor. Even he looks.

Walking down the middle of the road, followed by a 38 bus, is a tall exotic Arab-looking man with curly hair and a wide smile.

His arms dance high at his sides as he directs the strings of the large, furry pink-and-black mouse that is leading now not one but two, three and four buses.

He stops adjacent to the bus stop.

'Get out the way will you, mate!' shouts a bus inspector.

'No, man, no, this is art!' sings a Nigerian man in a swirling print green-and-gold shirt.

A few schoolboys clap, and the little black lady brings her hands together, 'Hallelujah! Hallelujah!'

The exotic man lifts his right hand and the red front feet of the mouse rise up and the mouse's head lurches from side to side. At the bus stop we crowd round as it begins to dance.

From the other side of the road, outside Marks and Spencer and McDonald's, people are watching. Soon there is a circle round the magic mouse. The man presses a button in a plastic bag and music serenades the dancing animal. It darts forward, backwards, and soon no one sees the strings because this mouse is alive!

A policeman taps the man on the shoulder. 'That's enough, don't you think, guv?'

The strings reappear; the mouse is folded into the bag.

I look down. The tip of the aluminium stick has left my toe, and the empty can of beer has been laid carefully against the bus shelter. Then Brillo-pad-hair man slips away, eating a slab of chocolate. His stick twinkles in the Mare Street sun.

Repairs

'Where's my car, Sheldon?'

He slipped out from under some rusting heap and big-smiled me as he lay on his back in the greasy yard. He took the lollipop from his mouth and clicked his fingers.

'Where's my car, Sheldon? You said five days, it's been three weeks.'

It was a yard of rusting heaps, most of them kept on the road with Sellotape, filler, sawdust and bribes to the MOT man.

Sheldon threw the lollipop stick into the corner of the yard.

'Had a real bad day?' he asked.

Strewn round the yard were big ends, twisted exhausts, tortured camshafts and treadless tyres.

'I need the car, Sheldon. Need it badly. I'm going away. Just get on with it, can't you!'

A small group of Sheldon's friends were sitting in a once powder-blue '78 Cadillac convertible that Sam had bought for restoration, though by now it looked well beyond any known form of revival.

Two of them lounged in the back of the once white-leather bench seat. The older of the two, with long dreadlocks and a Rasta band round his head, stared at me as he licked tobacco from his lips.

Don't look at me like that, mate, I thought, it's Sheldon you should be eyeballing, he never does anything, he just...

Oh bugger all this. I was hit by the misery of the early autumn late afternoon, this gory strewn-with-death vehicular world. By life. Hackney. The coming-millennium blues.

'You had a real bad day,' Sheldon said. 'I see that.'

I sighed. Sheldon yawned, smiled again, picked up a spanner and slid beneath the C reg rust-red XJ6 and banged on the sump.

'I need my bloody car!'

King Rasta in the back of the Cadillac scratched his chin, lent over the front seat, rummaged with his long fingers in the wide glove compartment and took out a perfectly shaped joint. He lay back, as grand as an African king, his white cowboy boots dangling over the front seat. He lit up and blew a perfume-cloud of smoke in my direction. The two other guys, younger and with shorter dreadlocks, wound themselves into coils of laughter. The one in the driving-seat twiddled the wheel with his left hand. Then he fished under the seat, pressed a button and Bob Marley's 'Rasta Man Vibrations' echoed up the curved windscreen of the Cadillac.

'Good smell,' I said.

'Too strong for honkies, man. Make 'em slip down holes,' said the king.

Sheldon came up for air from under the XJ6 and sat carefully against the rear door.

'Give 'im a blow, Daniel. Get him off my back!'

Daniel looked in the opposite direction.

'Daniel! Give me and 'im a big break.'

Daniel shook his Rasta locks slowly like a lion's mane.

'You a lucky man me in such good humour, Mr Sheldon, troubled as me be by all de cares of Babylon.'

He tapped his minion in the driving seat on the shoulder. The minion pulled out four joints from the glove compartment and arranged them for him on the palm of his hand.

The King selected one and called me over. As I walked across the yard, I avoided the slicks of oil, and kicked a used oil filter into oblivion.

'Dat de way, Mr lily-white Englishman. You take out aggression on dat filter, not on we poor subjects of de great British Empire.'

His sidekicks whooped. The King lay the single joint on his open palm like a gift from a pharaoh. I took it humbly. He struck a match for me.

'You light it right. Dis de finest Jamaica grass.'

'Thanks,' I said. 'I appreciate this.'

The yard changed colour slowly. The sumps and filters and tyres became exotic fruits on a tropical beach.

'Give a little space to our white brother, Winston,' the king said.

I slipped in the back seat between them and looked up at a bright blue sky and listened to Marley's positive vibrations.

I smiled at the King. He patted me on the shoulder.

'Maybe you a real black man in one lifetime. You ever tink dat, honky?'

Commodity Prisons

'The credit card was repor'ed missin', not stolen, innit?' she said to the two large security men as she stood at the front of the supermarket Help Desk queue.

The white girl was smartly dressed in a short black skirt, black tights and shoes, a silky blouse.

'Let me go!' she shouted to the security men on either side of her, and clutched her Gucci-style bag to her stomach.

I was standing towards the back of the Help-Desk queue, along with other disgruntled Hackney shoppers. I was holding my large, plump organic chicken, which I had bought earlier in the day, as it had been knocked down to half-price. But when I got home I realized I had been charged the full price.

We wish all our customers a Very Merry Christmas a cheerful female voice said through the sound system.

From the back of the store, a thin young man wearing dark trousers, blue shirt, tie, identity badge, walked down one of the aisles and straight up to the girl.

The two security men stood a few paces back.

The young man put his face close to the girl.

She was smiling at him.

Do you have enough wrapping paper for Christmas? the speakers asked us.

The supermarket official said loudly, 'We told you never to come to this store again.'

Her lipstick was dark red. Then she smiled again.

He went on, 'Are you stupid or something?'

We all watched like sly viewers of a dirty film.

This year we are offering our customers a truly international Christmas – dates from Morocco, wines for dessert from Portugal, cold meats with a difference from Spain, the sweetest Californian sultanas, not forgetting top-quality sirloin steaks from Scotland, or stilton and real apple cider from Somerset – and everything at our super-competitive seasonal prices.

'That's nice, innit?' she laughed.

She looked at me for a moment with unblinking eyes. I've seen through you, she seemed to say.

I gazed up the aisles stuffed with shiny goods of every shape. Huge trolleys were being pushed up the motorway-straight aisles. Those with the most bulging trolleys looked the happiest.

Jingle bells, jingle bells jingle all the way.

'Come with us to the office!' the official said.

'I ain't done nothing.'

One of the security men grabbed her arm.

'Get off me!' She slid to the floor, cradling her knees against her stomach, her short dress hugging her thighs.

'This way!' the young man shouted.

'I ain't going nowhere.' She placed her handbag across her knees.

May we remind our customers that our luxury 900g Christmas Puddings are sold with a free miniature bottle of Coburn's port.

The security men lifted the sitting girl and carried her up an aisle to the back of the store.

'Let go, bastards!'

Her kicking left leg dislodged a stack of Festive Xmas Crackers.

Comfort and joy, comfort and joy, great tidings of comfort and joy.

Soon I was at the front of the queue.

'Yes,' the assistant said coldly.

'You overcharged me for my organic chicken.'

'Do you have the receipt?'

I handed it to her. She showed it to another assistant.

In grudging silence she handed me the money.

The first Noël, the angel did say...

Outside, I checked the money and realized that the assistant had refunded me the price of the whole chicken, and not just the amount I had been overcharged. I turned round. No, no, I couldn't face that place again.

At home I put my free organic chicken on the carving board and made a herby stuffing, which I shoved up the bird, finishing off with a whole apple. I stared at the apple-stuffed end of the chicken, which turned into mocking lips: 'You won that one, innit?' the dark red mouth said.

Political Correction

In the run-down Bethnal Green side street the bright DIY shop front sparkled with vivid improve-your-home products. I too felt sparkly in my shock-purple shirt and white Levis. It was a long, thin shop, with stacks of shelves on either side and down the middle. The neon lights intensified the shiny products and made me blink.

The lettering of the names – 'Brillo', 'Rustin's', 'Dulux', 'Sandtex', 'Cuprinol' – were strained and cracked. Small scratches down the front of the Cuprinol 5 litre tin, a missing section on the 'D' of Dulux, were conspicuous under the lights. I searched the shelves for 'Wheeler's Traditional Beeswax Polish for Furniture'. There was an odd smell everywhere, like paint stripper mixed with disinfectant.

'Any Wheeler's Furniture Polish, mate?' I called out to the man at the counter.

He stood up straight. His straggly cream jumper revealed a large hole in the right sleeve, which showed his black shirt, making his elbow look like an old-fashioned air-gun target. His head twisted upwards. 'Don't sell much of that.' His head cranked itself down again and he studied the *Sun.*

I read the labels on a lower shelf, 'Goddard's Silver Polish', 'Brasso Long Life Protection', 'Warren's Blacking Polish'…

Slow boot-steps trod up the aisle at the other side of the high middle stack of shelves. A brawny hand touched the back of my neck, while another hand stretched round my shoulder. His finger pointed rudely – 'Wh-ee-lers Fur-nit-ure Pol-ish,' the gravelly cockney voice said.

'Thank you.'

He was a tall, cropped-haired skinhead.

'The last tin, how lucky,' I said.

'Lucky for some, innit.'

At the counter, the man smiled sourly.

A woman came out from the back of the shop. She was short, blonde and very made-up, tight jeans stretching round her waist. A large Union Jack was pinned to the wall behind her.

She looked at me, then at the skinhead. 'Middle class people buy all the 'ouses, that's what you think, innit, Jim?'

'Yeah,' Jim said.

The man at the counter stared at me.

'How much do I owe you?'

He picked up my jar of polish and tightened the lid.

'Strong grip,' I said. 'How much?'

Now the boy with the skinhead haircut rolled up his sleeves and revealed a large coloured swastika of Adolf Hitler.

My knees wobbled.

He raised his other arm, 'BNP'.

The man handed me my change. 'Not just niggers we hate,' he whispered.

I ran into the street before I was melted down and placed in some category on a shelf.

Lamb's Conduit Street

It is my favourite storm drain from which to hear the stories of the other London. Last week, after a storm, long after midnight, there was a lull in the traffic. I spread-eagled myself n across the thick, iron drain-cover. The roar from the secret river filled my mind.

I glanced up: 'A. France, Funeral Directors' glowed darkly. Opposite the undertaker, in a sort of graphic-design shop, there was a photograph of ex-President Clinton playing the trumpet. Outside the shop, a young man sucked a lollipop and tapped his lizard-skin-looking creepers on the pavement.

The unspoilt top-half of the Georgian buildings seemed to slope into the street. I heard sounds of water, like the splashing of a thousand dark fountains, flushing away the sins of London towards Coram Fields. Where does this great spring come from? Is it a conduit of the old river Fleet that ran through 'Hole Bourne' and then into Fleet Street?

I pressed my ear closer to the drain and the grills branded a shape on my face. The street stayed empty. After twenty minutes of this therapy the pressures of the city dissolve. Sometimes I believe I hear a scream or babblings down there. From my back pocket I took out 'The Magus', a card from the Aleister Crowley pack of tarot cards. I slid it between the grills of the drain and chanted the words of a Cabbalistic spell.

Two policemen turned the corner into Lamb's Conduit Street. 'Hoy, you!'

My black clothes faded into the night as I sped away.

The left side of my face is still warm: I had put my ear to the seashell of the city.

The London Library

It is worth the annual subscription to this fine private lending library, founded in 1841. It makes you feel you're almost there, a real writer.

Up the stairs, the balustrade of polished mahogany, on the wall portraits of Great People with connections to the London Library: Dame Rebecca West, Rupert Hart-Davis, Rudyard Kipling and many other past readers.

More mahogany in the elegant reading-room, the large window delicately sectioned, the eyes of readers like bees over their honey pots. I find a chair in an alcove and then take a number of books from the shelves. They smell fresh and green, not like the arid sterility of the tomes in the university libraries, where I pored over them, an anxious student.

Who is that over there? It is Richard Ingrams. And isn't that Andrew Roberts? Over there, Margaret Drabble. Well, here I am. I sit down again, sweep a little dust from the desk, practise my autograph on the blank page.

Restless, I duck and dive amongst the delightful reference books: *Whitaker's Almanac 1993*, *Who's Who 1999*, *The Guide to British Birds*. I finally settle in a brown-leather armchair in the corner and peruse the 1997 *Supplement to the Oxford English Dictionary*. As I sink into the chair, I begin to feel small.

I can't spell, I can't write, I can't do syntax, I'm a dud at etymology, semantics, analysing a sentence, having an original thought. Yet here I am.

One Great One taps another on the shoulder, a knowing laugh, a squeeze.

I retreat into the silent labyrinths, thousands of beautifully bound volumes, the calm, the long journey ended. I would like to die now and have my flesh and bones transformed into a book cover. Inside there will be one pure white page of finest hand-made vellum. Each year on my birthday a new librarian would be allowed to place me anywhere on any shelf in the London Library.

Framed

On the threshold of the Friends' Room at the Royal Academy I felt the London winter sales crowds pulling me back to the streets. Inside, a group of well-dressed women discussed the merits of the exhibition. Around the walls of the Friends' Room, a vivid display of paintings and drawings, with bold Fauvist backgrounds of primary colours, highlighted the almost-undressed Asian men and women. The county ladies, in their quietly pastel tweeds, remained unruffled by this display of eroticism. The women sank on to the dark leather sofas. The polished mahogany tables glowed with innate dignity. The hands of the county ladies were relaxed as they sipped their coffee, and I looked at their well-applied makeup and calm unblinking eyes.

A band of light crossed my eyes, from a thin brass strip, which stretched across the top of a black patent-leather handbag from one of the women opposite.

I smiled at the proud, elderly woman, her white hair perfectly coiffured and lightly permed. She turned away, revealing her long neck and suggesting the posture of a horsewoman. She looked at her friend: 'I shall be in Wiltshire until June.' A green enamelled brooch, of two birds, sparkled on her shoulder. Her bag was now resting diagonally across her lap.

I smelt perfume – my mother's perfume – and her gloved hand seemed to reach towards me from the sofa. I closely observed the woman's bag, which was the same kind as my mother used to like. I could see my reflection in its black patent shine.

'You've dropped your powder,' I said as she got up to leave.

'Thank you so much.' She picked up the compact.

The pressure of the sales crowds no longer tugged me. I imagined the woman putting down her handbag in the quiet of her house, my image embossed upon it.

Poetry Power

It is a February morning and I sit overlooking the Thames at a desk in the South Bank Poetry Library. The river, the sky, the dull hue of the buildings, pull me towards a London melancholy.

I try to tap out with my finger the rhythm of a poem I am writing, but I can't pick up the beat. Small waves swell against the pillars of Hungerford Bridge, others pitch on the two dark barges going downstream. Larger ripples roll on to the banks. This morning I feel lost in the midst of all the loud and confident syllables around me.

A mile to the east, in the City on the other side of the river, they are endlessly shifting the digits of money and power. Brokers and traders are tracing on their computer screens the moving prices of stocks and shares, commodities and futures, and money: dollars, pounds, yen, francs, euros, and the rest. Over the City, the grey sky looks brighter as if silver tickertape is dancing behind its clouds.

I tap all my fingers in irritation and give up. I find a poetry magazine on the shelves. Reading the text, any text, calms me briefly. You can't stop the tickertape of money, power, wealth. Poetry offers no competition. Poets are like an army of Quakers, sincere but impotent.

But this morning I smile at the bronze statue of Dylan Thomas by Olaf de Wet, which is in the entrance to the Poetry Library. A fag hangs from Dylan's mouth, his tie is loose, his head itself seems slightly distended, as if his energy was shaping the direction of his head upwards, towards heaven. Cheers, Dylan!

Big Boots

His black leather cowboy boots stretched on to the chair in front of him.

I welcomed the new batch of American students to my class at Birkbeck. I gave them handouts of the course I was teaching, 'London in Literature, 1837-1984.'

The cold bright January day lit the Keynes Library at 46 Gordon Square. Above the fireplace Vanessa Bell's painting glowed in its soft pastel shades. Virginia Woolf and John Maynard Keynes had both lived here.

The student's boots creaked. In the painting two men were sitting in armchairs; one was wearing light-purple slippers, with a huge book resting on his lap, while the other was leaning forward. They were engrossed in discussion as they sipped red wine. This was probably the room they were sitting in when the artist painted them and their presence comforted me.

The first name I called out on the register was 'Bret Atlas.'

His black hair was slicked back and shiny.

'Your surname is the name of a classic English motorbike,' I tried.

'So? It's an old American family name.' He propped himself on his elbows and his boots slid to the floor. 'British bikes are dead.'

A few students laughed nervously, some turned away, the rest stayed oddly still. As Bret sat back, the boots re-established themselves on the chair, the Cuban heels tilting towards me.

So the first class began: the background to the Great Exhibition, the decadent 1890s, Modernism, the students' feelings about Victorian London.

'What do you imagine Dickens's London was like, Bret?'

'Real smelly,' he said, 'and way too old-fashioned for my liking.'

'What do you like?'

'Women,' he leered, 'and big cars.' He scanned his audience. 'Everything in England is too small.'

'And too polite...?'

The muted colours of the painting seemed to fade even more.

The class discussion broadened. I set the reading and the seminar topic for next week. The students left. 'Good afternoon, gentlemen,' I called out to the chaps in the painting.

By the middle of term my relationship with Bret Atlas had gone well enough. He had picked up a sidekick, John Hew, who was like a baddy in a cowboy film. Bret always stayed just this side of overt rudeness. He handed in his papers on time too, throwaway stuff, but never bad enough to fail.

He had black, brown and white cowboy boots, which he wore for my class in that sequence. He teamed the boots with three thick leather cowboy belts, black, brown, white, which he always contrasted with the colour of his boots. He wore expensive blue jeans and good-quality buttoned-down corduroy shirts, white, black, green.

Before the start of the fifth class, in the corridor outside the room, a fluffy, pretty American girl with tight jeans and hugging white sweater, was sobbing.

'Look Bret, I won't be treated like that.'

'Honey,' he said, 'come on now.'

Other students were arriving and I went into the classroom.

Bret came in late, and combed the sides of his hair with a tortoiseshell comb. His face was more mobile than usual, and he scratched his back. As I talked about the historical background to Sherlock Holmes's *Sign of the Four*, he shared a joke with his chum.

His white boots hoisted themselves onto the chair, and he crossed his legs.

'Would you mind taking your feet off the chair, Bret? You're putting mud on it.'

He smirked.

'It's up to you,' I said, 'if you care so little for the students who have to sit there after your boots have left.'

There was a tense silence – but he kept his boots there.

In the classes after that, his boots had learnt better manners and only on a few occasions did they briefly take up their forward position.

In the class before the midterm break he sniffed me: 'I know that smell, Penhaligon's Blenheim Bouquet, my dad has it shipped over to Texas.'

'That's amazing!' I imagined a tanker loading up at the docks with his father's English aftershave.

'Where are you going at midterm, Bret?'

'I'm of to Paris with a friend, I've hired a pink Cadillac, going to drive around the place.'

There was a discussion that week about the different kinds of influence London had on the writers who lived here.

'What do you think then, Bret?' I pointed to the painting, 'of that bit of Bloomsbury culture?'

'Just old,' he said, 'everything about it is just old, and sort of finished. What's the point of those guys?'

He returned from Paris with photos of him and his friend driving around Paris and the countryside. Bret and the pink Cadillac were in the foreground of every shot.

Term ended. The two men in the painting appeared more relaxed, in their solid wooden frame, as they discussed art and books for eternity.

Sixteen years later, I still remember Bret, although the other students in that class have returned to blankness. Once I had a dream about him. He was in the pink Cadillac driving down a long road out of Paris. When I woke the scene brought to mind the Wim Wenders film, *Paris, Texas*, that wonderful story of landscape, struggle, beauty and travel. Although there was never any romance about Bret, the image made me think of him.

Email Faith

No new messages, was I too forward in my email, and where is the reply from my potential agent, has she got the stuff? The whole novel she's reading, she's just off Goodge Street, I've always liked that area, a good omen, and God that writer I met last night at the party, the working-class hero one, but in the end we got on well, and what awful paintings they were at that Mayfair Gallery where they held the party. Anyway I emailed him, and then he replied and I sent him the synopsis of my short story collection that he asked for. Did he hate it? – *No new messages* – how long since I last checked, well one does worry, and why has the lecturer not got back from Birkbeck about the first fifty pages of my novel? And no I'll never hear from the literary editor at the *Sunday Telegraph* again. Oh, it's all so hard, and for Jesus sake there must be someone out there who loves me and wants to make me whole and perfect. *No new messages*

The Party

I squeezed between two gorgeous women on the fuchsia-lined path and followed my friend-of-a-friend. He was going to introduce me to a chum of his who was something in publishing, who knew someone in New York who may want to read my novel.

'Steak?' asked a Friar Tuck figure from the midst of barbecue smoke, 'I'm Guy.'

'Simon.'

'You're Sophie's new partner…'

'No, I'm…'

'Thought you were.'

Sizzling drowned my words.

The thick steak sat on the plate I was carrying and I tried to keep up with my friend-of-a-friend as he veered towards the brick patio, but he was waylaid near the shrubbery by a younger woman, all blonde and breasts and legs. He was freshly divorced.

I slumped dejectedly onto a tartan rug, savoured my juicy steak and sipped Rioja.

'Mind if I sit down?' A ruddy faced ex-Major-sort-of-chap, his MCC tie smudged with red wine, plopped himself next to me. He extended a porky hand, 'My wife mentioned you. I'm Freddie…'

'Ahh…'

'Very good chap she said, if we need a new stockbroker, you're the ticket…'

'Actually…'

Chinese lanterns above us created floaty patterns on the grass and made me dizzy.

'I suppose they're all Conservatives here,' the Major said, 'but they talk bollocks, no backbone. Thatcher had more balls than the lot of them, as for the new one, too smooth.'

'Well...'

'I'm Audrey's father. What do you think of the wine?'

'Lovely.'

'The Rioja?'

'Yes.'

'That's mine, brought them a case, help them along, damn hard, those school fees, and three of them, poor blighters.'

'Are you staying the weekend?'

'Just a month or two, wife dead now.' He stared at the illuminated shrubbery as if he had seen a vision. 'Thinking of buying near here, grandpa flat, Shropshire's too cold, don't shoot any more, bones too brittle to hunt, you know...' He stared as if he had seen me for the first time. 'Audrey said you're an architect, very pleased to meet you.'

'Er, well...' I retreated to the edge of the rug.

A woman came down the path. 'There you are, Daddy.'

She leant down. 'Daddy needs his medicine,' she whispered.

'Quite understand,' I said.

Over at the shrubbery a Rizzla-paper distance separated my friend-of-a-friend and the blonde breasts-and-legs girl.

'Jeff, hello,' I called out cheerily.

Behind his back his arm flapped me away.

'Hoy there, young man!' The old Major waved his stick at me.

I retreated to the corner of the flowerbed and sat in a deckchair.

'Sorree, sorree,' my friend-of-a-friend came over, reeking of aftershave, and kissing a scrap of paper which he slipped into his top pocket.

'Another scalp?' I said sourly.

'Not her scalp I'm after, old boy.' He glanced up the path. 'There's your contact! Chas, Chas!'

Chas, short with a black suit, open-neck white shirt, gleaming bald head and big, round tortoiseshell glasses, held out his hand in a pumping motion as he advanced towards me.

'Hello,' I stuttered.

His handshake pulverised me. 'Heard about it,' he said, 'great idea,' his voice a New York rasp, 'A Hackney cookery book…'

'No…'

'Don't be modest, all that working-class tradition, aristocrats in the eighteenth century, the market gardening angle, then ethnic diversity! Great idea, I've seen you on TV, love your restaurant…'

An idiot smile stuck to my face.

'We'll talk business later, take my card, lunch is on me. Ciao.' He powered off like an expensive yacht.

The Friar Tuck host swayed towards me. 'Gather you're in banking. Can we have a chat?'

Home Match
2000 and beyond

Myfanwy, China, Harry, and a Goldfish

On August 19, 2000 my wife toked on the oxygen thingy above the bed, and so did I. It was a long, hard labour in the maternity suite at Homerton hospital. My anxieties were partly displaced by the first bunch of books I had been sent by Stephanie Merritt, who was then deputy literary editor of *The Observer*, for their short reviews section. I worked my way through one as I sat by Nicola.

Eventually the slow, painful movement of the birth began, and at about 8pm this slimy, wriggly, nicely featured little thing slopped out, cried wildly and nestled on Nicola's breast. Amazing that this child was *there* when a few minutes ago she was nowhere. We had already chosen her name: 'Myfanwy'.

Myfanwy curled into Nicola's arms while the hands of the handsome African consultant dived between my wife's legs until he had stitched her together again.

A few hours later, happy and exhausted, I went home and devoured a rare steak, salad, crusty bread, Camembert, and a good bottle of red burgundy. Too late to make phone calls, thank God, and I fell into a sleep of new-life vibrations and contentment.

The ringing phone pierced my brain.

'I'm in trouble. Can you come over?'

'Harry? It's six o'clock, I've just had a baby.'

In the total relief of knowing it wasn't the hospital, my headache announced itself with a thud, and helping Harry, one of my closest friends, seemed impossible.

'I've got to see baby! I can't just drop everything…'

'Please. She threw my goldfish out of the window, she won't leave, and says I am threatening to kill her.'

The usually cool-and-rational Harry was in a state.

Having checked that mother and child were fine, I arrived at Harry's ex-council fifth-floor flat in Southgate. Another old friend of his was there, Carol Dixon, a doctor.

Lin, Harry's Chinese girlfriend, said: 'Harry is keeping me prisoner.' Dressed in black trousers and green top, she was in constant motion, her long dark hair swishing across her face, bare feet scudding over the floor, eyes darting in every direction. She looked at us as if we were actors in a play. Carol spoke to Lin alone for half-an-hour.

Harry's eyes were like those of a weary old man. Apparently, everything had been fine until Lin saw a programme about Shanghai on the television – 'I don't want to be in gaol here, I must go home to China.' Then she had screamed piercingly.

Later that day Lin's Chinese friend, Huiliang, told Harry that Lin had been like this on a number of occasions in the last year. All Harry wanted now was for Lin to jump in a minicab with her luggage, to arrive at the airport and get on the plane to China. Her parents and cousins were waiting there to help.

Carol phoned doctors and hospitals and sounded very professional. No one was prepared to come out and see the situation for themselves. Lin was now tearing up strips of A4 paper into ever-smaller bits.

Harry peered over the balcony, 'She threw my goldfish....' The round goldfish bowl was next to the sink. Harry swivelled his finger round the empty bowl.

From the bathroom Lin shrieked: 'I'm going to stay here forever. I won't let them kill me.' Carol persuaded her to come out. We all had coffee and biscuits and nothing changed.

'I must get back soon,' I said, 'my baby, you know – why not phone the Chinese embassy?'

Carol pointed out politely that there were a lot of Chinese people in the world and why would they come out to Southgate to see a distressed Chinese woman? She phoned the embassy.

I went home.

Two days later a Mercedes from the Chinese embassy came and took Lin and put her on a plane to China. It turned out that her father was a senior official in the Chinese government. Two weeks later, on 3 September 2000, my Paperback reviews came out in *The Observer*. The first review was *Mao* by Jonathan Spence and I wrote in the last paragraph: 'The Cultural Revolution increased the repression in China. Spence calls Mao "The Lord of Misrule": this readable study explains why.'

It was one of those odd zen sequences.

Me and My Baby in London Fields

'Time for a walk, baby?'

'Is that wise?' Nicola says.

'Nature is good for a fourteen-week-old baby.'

Before Nicola can stop us, I wrap up Myfanwy and bundle her in to her eight-wheel-drive buggy with independent suspension. It is a blustery autumn day. I place a sort of elastic polythene bag over the front of the buggy, put up my green umbrella and we are off.

Through St John's churchyard we splosh, the umbrella veering dangerously in the west wind. The leaves from the London plane trees are thick on the ground, shades of yellow and red, and mix with sweet packets and McDonalds' cartons. But Myfanwy and I forgive all litter today.

The puddles are deep in Mare Street. By the railway bridge a car splashes my leg.

The buggy's suspension comes into its own over Hackney's Third World pavements. We cross by the traffic lights near the Town Hall. A schoolgirl peeps into the buggy. 'Ahh', she coos. And a stooped old lady carrying two bags of shopping gives us a smile soft with memories.

Myfanwy is gorgeous, Myfanwy is fine. Indeed she is the most perfect baby in Hackney, in London, in Britain, the universe.

The clumps of massed multi-coloured litter dance prettily between the traffic lights. The tips of my umbrella stretch upwards like stars in the wind. Myfanwy and her buggy cruise across the road into the Town Hall Square.

A cockney wino calls out 'Lovely baby, guv', comes over to the buggy and gargles at Myfanwy as he raises his

Special Brew in salutation. He looks into me and his beady eyes clear of all deception: 'I 'ad a lovely baby once.'

The square is filled with discarded Socialist Worker banners proclaiming 'Support for all Hackney Workers' and 'Tax the Rich'. Myfanwy burps.

We reach the Pub on the Park and I wonder if we should stop here and Daddy could sip a Guinness and twiddle baby in the baby area.

No! The gale force wind is a challenge and we carry on. The rain is like a million silver buttons on Myfanwy's rain cover. She smiles a rainbow smile. She is my child of wind and storms. She blinks. Her eyes are silver drops of rain with a centre of blue sea.

There is a smashed-up black Mondeo by the entrance to London Fields, and the rear door flaps open like a scar. I kick it shut and we pass into London Fields where the dignity of rows of trees along straight paths brings form and order to the scene.

As we tread along the path I have a sudden vision of another world, of sea spray in Swansea, of seaweed, and gulls twisting in air.... Should we have had Myfanwy in this mad inner-city world?

Yes, yes, yes! blow the trees. The rain sings like cymbals on Myfanwy's rain cover, her little legs and feet are fluttering leaves.

Now the storm sings and whooshes us up the path as the umbrella fills with wind. Myfanwy smiles as we leave the ground to float over London Fields.

Psychedelic Crayons

'Crayons, Daddy!' Myfanwy said, 'crayons.'

Myfanwy stared at the bright orange arrows and vivid green squares on the footpath.

These colours were so bright under the Mediterranean-blue Hackney sky that the middle-class family man peeled off like an onion, to reveal the hippy consciousness of my Welsh days, organic food, my flat that overlooked the sea in Borth, distant Snowdonia, drugs and dreams.

We held hands in our little paradise – to the east through the railway arch, the grinding traffic of Morning Lane, to the west the noisy convoy of buses on Mare Street, to the north the 'Murder Mile of London' where the drugs gangs shoot each other – but this was St John's churchyard, green foliage and tranquillity.

Myfanwy traced a yellow arrow with her left foot.

'Naughty,' she said, 'crayons in crayon book.'

'Very naughty. Come on, nursery.'

Of course signs on the pavement were the marks for gas workers, water pipe layers, Cable TV layers, and the others who make holes in roads. I sighed at the cold logicality of it all.

Next day there were more yellow stars, and green squiggles and circles from an urban Welsh wizard. Thousands of old hippies will swagger up Morning Lane, the men with hoes, flowers, and beards, the bra-less women in long tie-dye skirts, all singing Joni Mitchell songs. They will restore our dreams and our organic vegetable plots. Perhaps this is the spot where they will meet.

'Fantastic colours!' I said.

But she was cross and smacked my hand because they had not crayoned in the crayon book but on the pavement. Soon men would begin their work making holes.

The next day I was in a more sombre mood and there was no Welsh wizard on the loose. All the same, Myfanwy and I stopped at Churchwell Path and examined the ground.

Incredible! The brightest orange spots had made halos round the yellow arrows, and a new convoy of orange stars had made a rainbow shape across the path.

'Naughty!' she said.

The next day I was full of anticipation as we walked towards Churchwell Path. All the symbols were still there. Perhaps there were new ones?

'Get your kiddie out of the way, will you mate.'

I turned from my revelry to face a huge skinhead in a white T-shirt and with muscles like tennis balls.

'What?'

'Gas, mate. Main Drains tomorrow, Cable, Thursday.'

'All of you?'

'Redevelopment.'

I picked up Myfanwy and we watched as a troupe of hole diggers marched under the railway arch, led by a man on a mini-digger machine.

'So much for Welsh wizards.'

'Sorry mate?'

That afternoon when I trudged back from the nursery with Myfanwy, the magic colours on the footpath had been replaced by a long thin gully. Chevron barriers, with the contractor's 'O'Holleran' on each one, were stopping us tripping into the hole.

'Colours gone,' Myfanwy said.

The man on the mechanical digger shovelled up another gash-load of rubble.

Closure

i.m. of St John's Nursery, Hackney, 1947-2002

Is this a holy thing to see
In a rich and fruitful land?

'Holy Thursday',
from *Songs of Experience*, William Blake, 1794

'I'll get your child for you.' She blocked my entrance to the nursery.

'I've got presents for the staff,' I said.

'I'll see they get them.' Her dark grey two-piece was crisp.

I had never seen her before and asked who she was but she looked away. The rippling notes of children's laughter sounded from the large walled garden at the back of the nursery.

'Get out of the way!'

She tottered and let me pass. I ran into the garden and noticed two other parents climbing over the wall.

Hackney Council had cheated us. St John's Nursery was the longest-established nursery in Hackney, founded in 1947 for the children of war widows. It was due to close in a day's time but the council had pre-empted our plan to hold a demonstration. I got to the front door. The council had planned well: a group of 'Security' men, some with thick tattoos on their arms, waited by the gate.

Charlie and Diana, the two parents who had done most to fight this closure, came in from the garden. 'Bastards!' Charlie said. I patted his shoulder. A number of parents and staff gathered in the foyer.

Charlie opened the palm of his hand to reveal a set of keys: 'One of the staff got them to me,' he whispered. Half-an hour later the staff had left, under threat of disciplinary action if they stayed. Some parents and children went too. The sixteen of us remaining, ten adults and six children, were determined to occupy the nursery. More council officials, who were probably from the newly privatised education sector, 'The Learning Trust', stood by the gate.

Charlie locked the glass-panelled door. Most of the adults assembled in the staff room to discuss tactics, while the children were taken to play in the garden.

Quick-marching feet on the path shocked us and we ran to the front door. A bunch of policemen in full riot gear were at the entrance gates.

'There's nothing they can do,' Charlie said.

He called to the policeman that we were occupying the nursery. Truncheons tapped on riot shields. 'May I speak to the policeman in charge?' Charlie asked.

We cheered.

An Inspector, young and fresh looking, came forward and agreed to a meeting. The riot-policemen stood back and he came in. 'It's best if I just speak to a couple of you,' he said. Charlie and I took him into the office. After negotiations, and a separate meeting between the Inspector and the council officials, the Inspector accepted our position and said we could stay. He went outside and we locked the door again.

The senior person from The Learning Trust, red-faced and cross, stomped to the front door. 'We propose to turn off the electricity supply,' he said.

'That will look good in the papers tomorrow, won't it?' I replied.

'We want the names of all the people who are illegally occupying the nursery.'

After a discussion Charlie told them we agreed to this.

The police disbanded, leaving a woman police constable at the gate.

The occupying parents and children went into the early-evening warmth of the garden. The giant oak tree in the middle felt like a protector against the police, the council and the traffic of Hackney. The vicarage was next door to the nursery, and we phoned the vicar, Dr John Pridmore, but he did not answer. (I had tried the previous week to engage him in our campaign but it was clear that he wanted nothing to do with it. He had asked me not to mention his name to the Church Commissioners, to whom I was writing, as they were the owners of the land – I made sure I did.) The large parish church towered over us.

My daughter and her friends played ring-a-ring-a-roses. One of the parents came into the garden carrying packets of fish-and-chips. We all ate together, and then played games on the big green lawn.

We had two lookouts along the wall of the nursery in case the security men tried anything. When I peered over they were leaving in two red Transit vans. 'Scum!' one of them screamed at us.

A full moon rose over the nursery garden and I leant against the oak tree and gazed at the stars in the sky. A photographer from one of the tabloids – we had phoned most of the papers – climbed over the fence.

The nursery was occupied for three days and then we handed it back to the council.

A week later, after an emergency meeting at which my wife had made an excellent speech, the council decided by a single vote to close the nursery.

That evening I was walking through the graveyard and noticed bright arc lights in the nursery. A gang of workmen was unloading wooden boards from a lorry. They carried them one-by-one into the nursery area. Other men banged the boards into place over all the windows and doors.

Fifi

A Spanish girl walked down the graveyard path towards Myfanwy and me. The green leaves and foliage were silky from the summer rain.

'How are you?' I said.

She smiled out of her beggar grime, hinting at prettiness before the heroin got her. Her usual pitch was outside Woolworth's. I often gave her a pound and we would chat about the book she was reading.

She asked if this was my daughter. I said yes and she said 'She is so beautiful.' Myfanwy jumped over the little wall and sat amongst the grass.

'I show her how to make daisy chains?' Fifi said.

'Her name is Myfanwy.'

They sat, and Fifi showed how to link the daisy stalks. It was warm and Fifi took off her jacket. Her short-sleeved black sweatshirt revealed injection marks.

She placed a finished daisy chain round Myfanwy's neck. They got up and did a jig.

'Must go now.' She put on her jacket with shaking hands.

'Goodbye,' we said.

That was last year.

Summer is coming again in the graveyard. Fifi has not been around for ages.

Swiss Mountain Air

I sit on a side bench in the dusty school gym and wait for Myfanwy to put things in her bag after the Tai Quando class. Parents shuffle around uneasily. A woman comes through the door, her stick tapping the ground. Slight in build, she looks better than last year: her brown hair is cut short, her dark trousers and white blouse spruce, trainers are new.

The stick is bright and varnished, the handle a natural shape, a hiking stick made from one piece of wood. Three metal emblems are pinned on the stick, signifying different places. My father had a stick like that. It stayed unused in the umbrella stand behind the front door.

She draws close to her child and asks flatly if she had had a good day. The fair-haired girl smiles, and so does the mother who is almost certainly younger than she looks. They stoop to pick up a sock and both of them stuff it in the school bag, and giggle.

Pasty-skinned, the mother stands up, still bending. Her head dips, her shoulders hunch over the stick. She looks withered in contrast to most of the young parents.

With the stick she probes under the bench for any missing items. The shaft glints in the light, she swizzles it to right and left with great efficiency, and looks at no one. Perhaps she worries that some of us remember how bedraggled and unkempt she was last year.

With a flourish she links arms with her daughter. The stick leads them across the dusty wilderness of the gym, into the playground and then home across the crowded roads of Hackney. The emblem at the top of the stick said 'Innsbruck' and showed blue sky, snowy peaks and sun.

Home Match

It's strange to be going back. This is Myfanwy's first big match, at White Hart Lane, but she won't boast about it at school. She's Man U there, along with many in Year Four, while the others are Arsenal. Perhaps Spurs will tempt her.

Boarding the train at Hackney Downs, Spurs supporters chat and jostle, I grab the one seat left, put Myf on my lap. I listen to the jokes, watch the faces, note the fashion, short bomber jackets, well-pressed chinos, Ben Sherman shirts, Levis, expensive trainers. Spurs fans always had style.

'How many stops, Dad?'

'Not many.'

Early May sun is watery on Hackney Marshes. The Lea canal sparkles darkly. Vegetation on the embankments is almost festive as it sways in the wind-pull of the wheels. Bright graffiti livens up the concrete skateboard park. From the train I see abandoned railway huts, an overgrown path that would once have been a road, a few ruined houses. I am pleased to be distracted.

'Bruce Grove, Dad.'

We get off and walk down the curving path. People drift past. Many of the shops have old-fashioned frontages. The sun covers everything and I feel happy.

'Which way, Dad?'

Walking along Tottenham High Road the sun maintains its cheeriness. A fine Georgian building suggests a once genteel Tottenham. The momentum of the fans sauntering up the road excites us both.

'Quite cheap, Dad.'

Myfanwy points to a stall of Tottenham scarves and shirts. As she already has Arsenal, Man U and Roma gear

I explain that she should perhaps develop a sense of real loyalty to one club.

'Oh Dad.'

I used to come from Egham, with two other boys I didn't know well, to see Tottenham play, from 1969 to 1971. The worst time was when I was just sixteen and had my first motorbike. I decided to go to an evening match, and found my way on to the North Circular and got lost. It began to rain, and rain, and rain. I was freezing.

We turn off the High Road into Scotland Green, a small road of little shops, Victorian terrace houses and two pubs. We go into the second one, The Two Brewers, with a sign over the door, 'For Home Fans Only'. The woodwork is painted in Spurs colours. Inside the large spartan bar Spurs supporters of every size and shape laugh and joke and drink. Their collective buzz vibrates, I buy drinks and crisps, we sit in the garden, then stand outside the pub. The road leads down to a river or canal. The scene feels out of time, as if this working-class community has been by-passed by the modern world. We head off.

'There's just time, Dad.'

Myfanwy leads me in to the Spurs shop, we mooch around, she finds a half-price Spurs baseball-style cap, white cotton, the nicest in the shop.

'Okay wretch,' I say, 'I'll buy it.'

When I came as a boy I was never part of anything, though I liked the football. But the worst time was on my motorbike, I couldn't find my way home, so cold, so wet. Eventually I saw 'North Circular', the bike was spluttering. When I got home the house was in darkness and I was so wretched I could only just get off the bike.

Mother was in bed and said nothing as I came in. Father had died six months before. I hobbled in to the bathroom, between my father's room and my mother's room.

Inside the stadium, climbing the stairs, the sound oomphs from the crowd, Myfanwy grips the programme. We find our seats, the players come out, she comments like a pro on a player she recognises from her Match Attax cards.

'Wow, Dad, wow!'

We watch absorbed, munch sandwiches and crisps. I feel at home. Not a great match, Spurs win 1-0, scored a second that was disallowed. As always, Spurs hint at brilliance but never fully deliver.

The bath filled up, I sobbed and like a Meccano model managed to get my body in the water, and after a long time I unfroze. When I looked around the bathroom, I thought of my Dad's spluttering morning cough, and hated the cold green tiles round the bath.

'Look at those West Brom fans, Myf,' I point to the stand opposite, 'even though they're relegated they still sing their hearts out.'

'Yeah, yeah.'

We walk back down the High Road.

'I'm Spurs now, really.'

The sky is very blue, the wind sharp. At a table two ex-Spurs players are signing copies of the programme.

'Is it free, Dad?'

I think it is and she lines up with her programme. Micky Hazard, who had been there as we walked to the game, is still smiling and says something nice to her. I don't recognise the other player. When we examine his autograph we can't decipher it. The hot dog stand tempts me but I think of my weight.

'Nice watch.'

She points in a jeweller's window.

'Oh Myf.'

She does need one. We go in, the bearded Greek owner makes my daughter laugh, she chooses a small rectangular watch, with a swirling light-blue face and a matching strap. She walks out, holding up her wrist.

I look straight down the road, which glows in the late-afternoon sun. I want to walk on to see where it leads. Myfanwy stands by the traffic lights at the junction and stretches her arm towards me.

'This way, Myf.' I put her hand in mine.

We get on the train, chatter, make a wrong connection, jump on a bus in Stoke Newington, and get home at seven.

Woman in an African Dress

We pour into the red 38 bendy bus on this sweaty day and it locks us in. Those standing grip tight. I am sitting in the seat behind the driver and the glass panel that separates him forces me to stare at my reflection. At a bus stop the doors open and a refreshing stream of wind curls round my legs.

An elegant African woman sits by me, wearing a traditional-style swirling yellow dress, so purely bright that it feels as if sunshine has entered my mind. As we head up the Essex Road her right arm knocks against mine, then again, and she guides it back to her lap with her other arm. 'It's stress,' she says in a strong, even voice, 'I'm sorry.'

'That's okay,' I say helplessly. She manages to use her mobile and talks in soft English, though I don't catch the words.

Her arm vibrates more violently. Near Islington the bus's air brakes hiss, and she speaks more desperately in an African language into her mobile. At the Angel she bundles things into her bag, squeezes my elbow and stands up. The beauty of her pure sun-yellow dress looks out of place.

She steps on to the hot pavement, her right arm repeatedly hitting her thigh.

The Thames Barrier

It was a stormy August day in Greenwich when I bought my ticket for the boat trip. The hanging baskets in the waiting area contained the deadest flowers I had ever seen. The wind turned my umbrella inside out.

The *Chay Blyth* was a cheerful little boat and bounced over the choppy swell as we left the quay. Although there used to be a palace at Greenwich and Wren's Royal Naval College is one of the finest buildings in London, there is nothing aristocratic about the Thames. The current of the brown river is a leveller, it echoes of time and death, as it slides towards the bleak Essex flatlands and the sea.

We headed up river. A one-legged man on crutches, one cavalry twill trouser leg folded up and held by two large brass safety pins, moves unsteadily along the wet deck, refusing all help. He sits at the front. The banks near Woolwich Reach, full of small factories, grim dwelling places and wasteland, speak of endurance rather than celebration.

The Thames Barrier, constructed between 1974 and 1982, has two main functions: to protect Londoners and their homes from flooding; to preserve the heritage of London, its art and architecture, theatres and libraries. Threats from flooding have increased drastically. Before 1990 the number of barrier closures was on average two per year. Since 1990 the average has been four per year. In January 2003 it was closed on fourteen occasions.

The overflowing of the Thames is not a new phenomenon. Samuel Pepys, in a diary entry of 1663, noted 'There was last night the greatest tide that ever was remembered in England to have been in this river, all Whitehall having been drowned'. Many Londoners died in the surge tides of 1928 and 1953.

The *Chay Blyth* moves into midstream and two Japanese girls squeal as white foam blows over them. Their cameras flash brightly. This melancholy day depresses me. In *Heart of Darkness* (1902) Conrad beautifully evokes the mood of the Thames at London, his characters in a boat at anchor: 'The air was dark above Gravesend and farther back still seemed condensed into a mournful gloom, brooding motionless over the biggest, and the greatest, town on earth.'

The Thames Barrier is a structure that endures all human emotion, as well as tides and floods. Words, sentences, selves, are flotsam in comparison to its solidity. The brilliance of the construction is a tribute to a great deal of behind-the-scenes work. The informative book, *The Thames Barrier* by Stuart Gilbert and Ray Horner (1984), is a mine of information. For example, there were thirty-seven people on the Policy Committee (set up in 1968) including those from organisations whose expertise is little known to the general public. There were many committees, including an 'Oceanographical and Meteorological Working Party'; a 'Pollution and Siltation Working Party'.

Rain beats on the flimsy awning across the passenger deck. A small group of hearty Australian men, wearing team scarves, jostle each other to get below deck and into the cafeteria. 'No wonder the Poms look so down, Jim,' he said to his friend.

The *Chay Blyth* draws near its objective. Most stand and try to make sense of the sight. The Australians come up from below decks with tea and cakes. 'They copied that from the Sydney Opera House!' one of them points to the shaped aluminium tops of the Barrier's gates. They look too like nuns' wimples, hinting that prayer and faith are helping to hold back the waters. Close up, the Thames Barrier is a fantastic piece of engineering. The boat stops for a while and I try to look knowledgeable as I examine the bits and pieces of the structure.

The range of materials used in building the Barrier illustrates a sophisticated technical world of which most of us know nothing. The adverts at the back of *The Thames Barrier* reveal an unusual world of things: trunnion shafts, special bearings, lifts, low-voltage switchgear; 'the Williamsform she-bolt system, a concrete formwork securing system'; 'Chockfast® (pourable epoxy chocks)'; 'Linatex rubber (it holds back the waters)'; pressure relief wells and ground anchorages.

Many photos are taken by those on board. The Japanese girls giggle. The one-legged man knocks a crutch hard on the ground and stares tight-lipped. As the boat pauses it wobbles disconcertingly. We move off again towards Greenwich. Rain sweeps across the boat as the silver tips of the barrier flash against the grey sky.

Abney Park N16

If you enter the cemetery from Church Street through the renovated entrance gates you find the perfectly-maintained monument to William Booth (1829-1912), social reformer and founder of the Salvation Army. His Christian soldiers are a good lot. Yet his sarcophagus no longer represents what this place is about. There are more powerful energies at work.

On a fine day you would not be aware of these forces. For this is the brightest of spaces. The trees make a harlequin's cloak across the acres of the dignified dead. Children, parents, young lovers, frolic between the shadows. Dogs, cats, squirrels, mice, wander cheerfully. Birds flourish. The winding paths takes you into such dense green spaces that you almost believe London no longer exists.

In a rainy autumn there is often the strange sense of being touched, by hanging branches, bushes, leaves, spiders' webs, slugs' slime. I once had the fear that if I stayed still too long I would be encased in ivy. On that occasion I was restored by the sight of a tomb to the Bostock family on which sat a finely carved lion. The inscription reads: 'In that happy Easter morning / All the graves the dead restore / Father, sister, and mother meet once more.' Tender love defies oblivion.

There is variety in the expressions of death. I notice on one headstone a well-preserved photograph of a dark haired, handsome woman. I fantasize that she is about to set out, on a Friday in late 1950s London, a Du Maurier between her fingers and fragrant from her weekend scent, for an evening of ballroom dancing. The reality of her perished flesh beneath the earth chills me. On a connecting path there is a small black marble memorial to two brothers, who both died in their twenties, in 1993 and 2002 respectively. Behind this is a sapling, to which a printed note is attached: 'Please stop stealing my flowers. You are upsetting me very much. I am David and Tom's mum, Margaret. Thank you.'

Although this place encourages reflection, one is also struck by bravado: in the face of death the Victorians developed the elegance and drama of mortality. The main entrance on Stoke Newington High Street has Egyptian-style gates, and the entrance drive is wide. After this there are a series of tall pillars, some with angels, others depicting a broken column. All of them are three times taller than the average man. Was this cultural tendency for excess due to a confidence in the afterlife or a terror that there may be nothing there?

This place is one of extreme contrasts. Behind the grand thoroughfares are secret areas where graves cluster together like snug hamlets. Such places are perfect for a quiet picnic or a lovers' tryst. Generally, there is a feeling of peace amongst the dead. As you read the names on the graves, 'Maeve Bowles', 'Lucy Turton', 'Charles Ryder', you feel part of a restful community. Yet a sense of disharmony is never far away. Recently I came across lurid pink handwriting scrawled over an old stone headstone: 'Here lies Popadom, May she rest in peace.'

Abney Park was a non-denominational cemetery laid out in the 1840s by a private company. In 1972 the owners were declared bankrupt, although unauthorized burials continued for a few more years. Hackney Council now has responsibility for the site. In 1974 the Save Abney Park Cemetery group was set up, and the volunteers of today originate from that beginning.

There are many dignitaries buried, or memorialized, here. Isaac Watts (1674-1748), poet, writer of hymns, headteacher, who was educated at the prestigious Non-conformist Stoke Newington Academy, is honoured by a huge statue, which was paid for by public subscription in 1845. A War Memorial gains in dignity through its understatement.

There is always the hint that chaos may break through. This anxiety is at its strongest in autumn or winter, especially after twilight. In certain spots nature has become unnaturally fecund: ivy hugs the curves of graves, tombs and benches. The moss is thick along the paths where weeds, fungi and graffiti struggle for dominance.

Once, a glue sniffer, a large young man with a skinhead haircut, his face stiff and his lips dribbling, jumped out of the bushes in front of me. Another time I passed on quickly as two people copulated noisily behind some trees.

In the middle of Abney Park is a chapel designed in the 1840s by the architect William Hosking, which combines elements of Gothic architecture with an overall geometric shape that is severe in its classicism. It is ruined now, closed to the public, and its roof is open to the elements. The presence of this building haunts the cemetery and to stand close to it, even on a sunny day, is to feel depressed. The ornate plasterwork of the tall Gothic windows is crumbling. Higher up, the four round, mandala-shaped windows have no glass in them although they would once have been a central aesthetic feature of the chapel. The spire, tall for such a small building, is intact and so are the spindly little turrets. So much effort came to this. Through the locked steel fence I can see dog shit, old clothes, rubble.

God has abandoned this building. There used to be occult symbols – a pentagram, an ankh, an upside down image of Christ on the Cross – painted onto the church. On a bench outside the chapel was the inscription: 'Do What Thou Wilt is the Whole of the Law', a quotation from Aleister Crowley, most evil of magicians.

In the 1980s there were articles in the local press about Satanists and witches holding ceremonies here (I gather there is still a group of black magicians practising their craft in the locality). These inscriptions have now been removed. Yet to stand here at night is to sense a force that is frightening.

As I walk out past the good General Booth I imagine the muted singing of hymns. The tinkling cymbals I half hear sound flimsy and far away. Death is dense and luscious in this place.

To Tony

i.m. Tony Halliday, 1945-2006

One of my neighbours killed himself. The strange thing was that he always felt like a ghost, as if your look passed through him. In London human presences are soon forgotten until out of the blue – that person is no longer here. Tony was an art historian, who some years ago had worked at the Courtauld Institute. Another neighbour, Audrey Brodhurst, a fierce intellectual old lady, who died ten years ago, had said that Tony knew about a few Aleister Crowley texts that were kept as secret as possible in the Courtauld Library. I had rehearsed many times the conversation I should have with Tony about this interesting point.

Spring-Cleaning the Ghosts

They are restoring the tombs in St John's churchyard, Hackney.

Each day the young stonemasons arrive like a little band of tomb priests. As they strip off the layers of dirt and flaky stone, the dead are reborn and then re-clothed in a lime wash solution.

The lucky ones have their lettering repainted, for example the exotic tomb of the Rivaz family. One inscription laments the loss of their son: 'Sacred to the memory of First Lieutenant Francis Clifton Rivaz of the Ist Bombay Fusiliers who died on board the *Oriental* in the Red sea on the 15th February 1855, aged 26 years.' Now his long death has been re-inscribed.

The crest of the aristocratic Cravens has a melancholy hue as if the family is discomposed to find itself in one of the poorest boroughs of London. Rear-Admiral Sir Francis Beaufort KB (1774-1857) exudes a greater confidence. Hackney Council's attached details about the origins of the Beaufort Scale confirm his resurgence. Thomas Edward Spencer (1845-1911), born in Hoxton, became president of the Stonemasons' Society at the age of twenty-four. The restorers retouch his memorial with professional courtesy.

The language of death has a quiet grandeur our age cannot emulate: 'Leaving an affectionate husband and twelve children to deplore their irreparable loss.'

As the world helter-skelters towards oblivion, how beautifully absurd is the love of these craftsmen for their work. They have no utilitarian purpose, and revel in restoring the past so that it flickers with dignity on the chaos of our present.

Today, graffiti was scrawled across the angel's wings on a finely ornamental tomb, but the insult felt inconsequential.

Beginnings

London Advances

In the 1960s the southern spread of London stopped and the country started at Egham. We lived near the railway station and I vowed at the age of eight never to be one of the trapped commuters. Our telephone number was Egham 9.

My head was full of soft country sounds. Any taint of the city dissolved as I turned into the road to Prune Hill. Mrs Caddie grazed her prize Jersey cows on the adjacent land, and her wide, lazy fields gave us mushrooms for free. Further up the road, the Shell Research Laboratory buildings were very modern, but they never took over the countryside. Beyond that, luxurious with trees, a hill led up to Royal Holloway College.

Nearby was a potholed track, at the end of which was a messy old farm. One Saturday in May, when I was eleven, the farmer charged over his muddy fields and shouted at my friend and me: 'Stop, boys, stop!' We ducked behind a thick hedge and crawled away from him.

'I'm not that slow!' His vulture's eyes stared at us over the hedge. 'You've been stealing birds' eggs.'

We hadn't. His big, plump body glowered at us, but I liked his voice. He had a real country accent, here, so close to London, as if the rhythms of this untroubled backwater had gurgled through him and his ancestors for centuries. London was far away on a hill, a place for dreams to come true or nightmares to be born.

This countryside was mine, where I messed about in trees, tangled with thistles, made bridges over rivulets, rolled in the long, secret grass. I looked out for the old people who kept up country ways.

When I was thirteen, Mrs Caddy took me into her farmhouse and gave me elevenses. 'Don't stare so!' she said. I needed to hold on to something, and believed with all the blurred intensity of early adolescence that my gaze would fix her in an eternal present. A few years later she died. Her cows were sold, and later her farm.

My mother referred to Egham as 'the village', and we seemed to know most people. In 1966, Marge was at the sweet shop, which hadn't changed for a hundred years; Mr Roberts was the optician, and he always wore a bow tie; Mr Anderson was the dentist, and he played golf with my father; John Chilvers was the butcher, and his fingers were as fat as his homemade sausages. On the corner of Station Road was the National Provincial Bank, where Mr Griffiths, the ruddy-cheeked cashier, usually dealt with my mother.

By the end of the 1960s Egham was being 'Redeveloped' – the heart of it was knocked down – to make way for new offices. One day I saw the old farmer in Coventry's, the newspaper shop. Behind his back, a couple of boys held their noses and laughed. That evening I quarrelled with my father. He was senior partner in a firm of chartered surveyors, Gale and Power, and he must have known about these developments. I told him it was disgraceful, he said I was rude.

Over the next few years all kinds of firms moved out of London to Egham and its hinterland. New roads were built. St Anne's Hill, only three miles away, which was a beautiful park, and The Old Mill, a magnificent old restaurant, were both destroyed. For a while the lane near the restaurant stayed visible.

One early morning I saw a 'For Sale' sign by the old farmer's boarded-up house. There were no sheep or cows anywhere. In a nearby field an ex-army lorry was parked. From the back of it, gypsies were unloading old carpets, washbasins, car tyres, an old bath. 'You can't do that!' I shouted. Two big boys jumped off the lorry and charged towards me. I was a quick runner and they didn't follow me onto the road.

The lorry left and I examined the mess. A rubber hose from a vacuum cleaner stuck out and swayed in the wind. I turned at the voice of the farmer, but it was only a gate rubbing on its hinges.

From a huge bag of paper I drew out a postcard with four photos on it: 'Sights of London'. I realised then that this junk was a kind of boundary; the advance London army was marking new ground.

Simon Carver Looks at Life

I've had an eventful time for a boy of thirteen years and two months. My life could nearly be a film already. I love films. In my room I've got posters of Cliff Richard's *Summer Holiday*, the Beatles' *A Hard Day's Night* – I saw these a couple of years ago – and *The Birds* which Mr Hitchcock signed for me. I'm playing *Sergeant Peppers Lonely Hearts Club Band*, the best record in the world. I love writing too. My life is a bit weird. This is what happened yesterday.

June 15, 1967

I felt great after the cricket match. My housemaster, who is also head of games at my prep school, stood in the door of the pavilion and bellowed, 'Well done Carver, that was first class, if you do that against Papplewick next week I'll give you your colours.'

'Thank you very much, sir.'

'And Carver,' he took his hands off the top of the pavilion door, and came over to me, filling up all the space he was so tall, 'we might still get you into Charterhouse if you go on playing like that.' He stared at me with his blue eyes and patted me hard on the back.

'Wow, great sir, certainly easier than common entrance.'

'Don't get too cocky, boy.'

I was taking common entrance next term and you had to be a real swot to get into Charterhouse. But as I was just thirteen I could always take it again. One of my friends who had been watching the cricket, Tubby Groves, came over to me and said, 'That was really great

Simon, forty-one, brilliant runs, fantastic.' He patted me on the back too.

'Even Matron clapped at one of your fours,' Hearson, the vice-captain said.

After showers I was combing my hair in the mirror and Miss Gifford, one of the sub-matrons, said, 'You'd better get your hair cut or you'll look like a film star, won't you?' I sort of laughed and went a bit red because she looked at me really nicely. My hair goes very fair in the summer and last holidays Rudd-Jones's sister said it looked great.

We always had a special tea after cricket, with the other side in the big hall, looking out at the cricket pitch, the tennis court and the headmaster's garden. I loved the look of the grounds in summer; everything was perfect every year, and always the same perfect, if you know what I mean. Alan, the groundsman, went past and put his thumbs up at me. That made me feel great. He loved cricket and knew everything about bats. I never wanted to go to public school. I just wanted to stay here and play cricket and touch Miss Gifford everywhere when she had no clothes on. I go stiff whenever I think about her.

I left school to go home on the train. I was happy except that my mother didn't come to watch me play. She normally does on a Saturday because we don't live far away. Everyone really liked her and my housemaster's ears always changed colour when he talked to her. And the headmaster used to come out of his study when he saw her and say, 'Er, how's that marvellous sports car, er, going, Mrs Carver?' When she looked at him and smiled you could tell it made him feel good because his arm started twitching. He always did that when he was pleased.

I bought a Mars Bar on Windsor and Eton Riverside station and looked for some girls to watch. If you looked closely you could sometimes see the tops of their legs and almost everything. As the train went past Datchet I wondered why my mother didn't come. I really liked her watching me play. Everything I did and even my fielding got quicker when she was there. A golfer hit a golf ball on Datchet golf course. I hated golf. Stupid little ball could go anywhere with a big hit. In cricket everything is skill, especially when you're a slow left arm spin bowler like me. But I don't always bowl because I'm even better as a batsman.

My mother used to be an actress. She was so good she could have gone to Hollywood, lots of people said that. My father, who is much older, and very ill, knew Mr Hitchcock quite well.

When I grow up I'm going to make films because I love looking at things and making different shapes with photographs and cine-films. I was in the photography club at school and my uncle Richard was going to buy me a really good camera at Christmas. Mother stopped acting when she had me. We live in a big house. My father doesn't work anymore but I think we're quite well off. My mother once said to me, 'Darling, you're always rich as long as there's enough money for a dry martini in the cocktail bar at The Savoy.' My father heard and told her off.

My mother got ill sometimes and drank a lot and shouted at me and wandered all over. When she was like this she never looked at me. Yesterday she was staring into the garden, 'The grass needs cutting, that bloody gardener.' But it had only been cut the day before and it looked beautiful. Sometimes I felt alone with this person who was my mother but not my mother. I wondered why she didn't come to watch me today.

I looked out of the train window at Staines. I knew Lindsey wouldn't be there because it was a Saturday. Lindsey went to a convent and I used to talk to her on the train going home. She teased me because she was a bit older and knew all about kissing and everything. One day, the train was quiet, she just said, 'Do you want to kiss me?'

'Okay, I suppose so.'

The first time our teeth knocked. We did it a few times in the next few weeks and it got good. Then she wasn't on the train anymore. One of her friends said that her mother had started to pick her up in the car. But I looked just in case.

It was getting cloudy. I wasn't that sad not to see Lindsey again. I'd gained a lot of experience and my friends at school were impressed. It was different with Paula Day. She was the sister of a boy at school. We used to write to other boys' sisters. She was at boarding school in Kent. Then I met her in the holidays. Justin Day was one of my good friends and I stayed with him and his family at their cottage in Wiltshire.

Paula and me liked each other straight away. She had short dark hair and looked brilliant in her tennis dress – she could play nearly as well as a boy. Justin got in a real bate with us. We couldn't help it. When we looked at each other, phew. I don't mean sex. I mean I looked at her and all the world went still. It just stopped. And you felt more fantastic than you ever did. Everything was perfect and still, like a game of cricket, no more, but you weren't afraid of anything when you looked at someone like that and they looked at you too. We did kiss and went further than ever but it was the looking that was really great.

Their father worked for Burmah Oil. Justin said, 'My father has to go to the Philippines to blow something up.' And they took Paula with them and sent her to an embassy school. That was three months ago. She hasn't written. And Justin won't give me her address. I can't stand him anymore. I'm not usually like that with friends.

When I got off the train I looked for my mother.

Sometimes she just arrived. She'd guess which train I was on. All the porters were very polite and friendly to her. But she wasn't here today. I needed to talk to my father about pocket money. He was good like that. We discussed things properly and worked out what was right and how much pocket money I should have and everything. 'You see old chap, you have to make a good argument to me and then we'll see.' He didn't do that much now because he was so ill and everything.

I walked round the block a few times because I felt a bit sick and funny. Too much match tea. I stopped outside our house. The long hedge, I think it is a laurel hedge, had been cut by our gardener, Bill Cranham. He always came on his bike with plants at the back. I called out 'Bill, Bill,' but no one was around. Our house was a big Victorian house with two huge windows at the front, which let in tons of light. My mother wanted to live on the Wentworth Estate where she had lived before she got married to my father. 'We're not living in Hollywood by the Lake,' my father told her.

I had to go inside.

'I'm home.'

There wasn't any sound. Even Pedro, my dog, didn't come out to say hello. My feet made masses of noise over the little tiles. They were mosaics or something. My mother had them put in. My stomach felt really bad now. It was always dark in the hallway, like being a prisoner in a huge dungeon. There was no one in the dining room or sitting room. I went through the long hallway to the kitchen.

'Darling, hello.' My mother's hand slipped from a tumbler of whisky and she puffed up her silk nightdress.

'What are you drinking now? You look horrible.'

'Oh do sit down, old chap.' My father spoke very slowly and the words came out muddled. His white hair needed combing and he'd spilt food down his polo shirt.

'Your nose is all red.' I stared at him and wanted to kick over his walking-frame. He was drinking whisky too. 'You look like a couple of alcoholics.'

'Oh, the thought police are home again,' my mother sneered. She tried to put a cigarette in her mouth, first on one side, and then the other. Her lips were cracked.

'I had a great game of cricket today, you know.'

'Oh God can't you think of anything but yourself?' She stared but didn't see me at all. Little veins throbbed in her cheeks.

'Why can't you tell her to stop drinking, Daddy, why not?'

'What a brilliant little drama queen.' My mother put her fists up at me.

'Shush, shush,' my father said. His eyes were hazy like they had a lace curtain over them. And he had a circle of white round his irises, which I'd never seen before.

'Shut up, both of you.' She flung her arms in the air and looked like she'd been kissed by Dracula. 'I'm going out.' She slammed the door and threw a glass in the hall. The sound spread over the mosaic floor. 'I hate that little bastard.'

I was afraid. I phoned Dr Taylor. It rang for ages but no one answered. The house felt empty. I was lonely and my father looked like he was about to be sent off to Madame Tussaud's. I don't think the lace curtains over his eyes were ever going to come down any more. Two years ago when she was last like this he looked at her slowly and seriously. She went a bit funny but later said she was going to cook a special meal for her 'two favourite men'.

Then I saw her rush across the back lawn. She had shoes on now and a mac but I could tell she was still wearing her nightdress. Where was she going? Why? My mouth was dry. I might never see her again. I followed her out of the back gate. It was nice being outside. It was still sunny and the light wind felt friendly. 'Mummy, why don't you come back, have a cup of tea and a chat with both of us, oh come on.'

She walked fast. 'Go away,' she flicked her hand at me. 'Go back to your cricket, you spoilt brat, I'm going for a long walk. Leave me alone.'

She shouted the last words so loud anyone could have heard. It was horrible. I couldn't think of films any more. She went towards Prune Hill. Luckily no one saw her and then she turned down a footpath. It got windier. I couldn't think any more about the nice day I'd had or my friends or girls or anything. I only had on my Aertex shirt and I was shivering.

'Please slow down a bit,' I pleaded. She turned round and threw stones at me. I stopped dead. 'Oh stop being so silly will you.'

She lifted her head slowly and tossed it back. Bits of hair escaped from her bow like corkscrews on either side of her face. 'Do you think it's silly, you stupid little boy,' she bent down and dug up a patch of weedy earth, 'to be yourself, to have to escape from all you bastards just to be yourself?'

She flung the earth at me and nearly tottered over. I cried now, not with all my face, but just loads of tears coming straight out of my eyes. I couldn't help it. She stared at me like I wasn't her son at all.

'You pathetic little boy.'

I couldn't say anything. She held her fist straight out in front of her and turned it round and round. Then she rushed off the footpath and into the waste ground. She fell over and got up. I could see she'd cut her knee. I couldn't move. I watched everything.

It was about seven now and wispy clouds were covering up the sun. My mother ran through the waste ground, fell over again and got up. She turned round. There were stinging nettles moving all around her. Yellow buttercups and straggling weedy things were shushing about in the wind. Behind the footpath, on Chambers Road, all kinds of trees were dodging in the wind. Mother's hair flew around. Everything was just moving. It was horrible. She shouted at me but I couldn't hear what she said. Nothing was ever going to stop doing all these separate things. I knew now that my mother was just doing what she had to do, like weeds and stinging nettles. I knew we were all weeds and stinging nettles. Houses and schools and cricket and love were all pretend. You could never stop everything going on just the way it had to. Not even in films. I felt really sick.

She doubled back and I followed her. She rushed into the station and then jumped on a train. She never looked round for me. I stood outside in the quiet by a tree. I was calmer but when I looked everything was different. I wish Paula Day had been here. I could have looked into her eyes. Then I was sad because it was probably all pretend.

'Monkeyface', the name we gave to one of the porters, came over to me. I'd never really liked him as much as the others. 'You look worried son.' He looked into my eyes. His teeth were yellow and cracked. He went on looking at me, like he really cared.

'Was that your mum? Don't worry, she's an actress, she'll be all right.'

I looked back at him. I think I might have smiled or blushed.

'Do you want a cup of tea?' He put one leg behind the other. 'I'm off now, I'll make you a nice cup of tea, shall I?' He nodded his big head up and down. 'You know I've got a famous train set, don't you?'

'Okay,' I smiled.

I thought of my father. I hoped he was dead when I got home. I didn't ever want to go home. Monkeyface really cared. The world felt all slow again. I wasn't so sick inside anymore.

A Lancashire Tale

In this starry winter night I sit in a striped-blue deckchair in my Hackney garden. Above, on the railway arches, a train stutters over the heavy sleepers. It sounds like the clogs of the Lancashire dead. That sound passes and now there is only the distinct clok-clok of a single pair of clogs. It is the ghost of my Lancashire mother. I hear her climbing over the railway arch and into my garden.

My mother's spirit does not rest because she is a ghost that is haunted. I feel her fingers stroke my hair.

Since her death ten years' ago she has visited me many times. For years before she died she would often say, 'Simon, I can never forgive my grandfather.'

But she would never say what it was he had done.

My mother sits next to me on the grass.

Beneath my garden lies one of the buried rivers of London. Tonight I hear it churn. I imagine it is a river running through a cavernous space that is like a coalmine.

Mother picks fretfully at the wet grass.

From the storm drain on my patio, I feel a presence rising, and I know it is my great-grandfather, Isaiah Piggott.

Something short and powerful seems to stand behind mother and me, as if it has just risen from the Wigan pit.

My great-grandfather stares at my mother, who has become a young woman again.

Now he stares at me.

He says, 'I was born in Low Green, near Wigan, 1842. Door boy, Wigan Colliery, 1853. I fought for the light. I came from nowhere, you mardy boy!'

He walks over and stands on one side of me. My mother stands up and stares at him over the top of my head.

He goes on, 'In 1850 when I was a right littl'un, Mr Fermor-Hesketh, with a pumping engine he designed himself, drained the water marshes round here. I loved watching him, and seeing the miracle of what a man can do with a machine. He used to give me sweets, but what he really gave me was the power to dream.'

My mother says, 'You only ever thought of yourself! My mother died when I was just thirteen. And my father, Hughie Piggott – your son – was always away somewhere, working for you. And when I was eleven my mother left him because he was cruel to her. You said my mother was a bad influence and made me live with a relative at Carlton House in Burscough Bridge. And my mother lived in a little cottage in Hoscar. You said I wasn't allowed to see her. But I used to run down the lane to leave letters hidden behind a secret tree for my mother.'

My great-grandfather stands up very straight and says to my mother: 'It weren't my fault what happened to your mother – my daughter-in-law – she had smallpox, it happened in them days.'

'She came to you for help,' mother says.

Great-grandfather frowns, 'She weren't family no more.'

'You were nothing but a greedy man!' my mother shouts.

I sense my great-grandfather tap me on the shoulder. He says to me, 'See that. Make a family of gentlefolk and that's how they treat yer!'

I feel his black-coal eyes burn into my neck.

He goes on, 'The Preston to Liverpool railway came through Burscough in 1849.'

My mother spits and says, 'So what! You killed my mother. And when you saw us flying a kite on Parbold Hill, you made her pull it in, and then you took it away.'

Great-grandfather is almost foaming at the mouth, 'I made the future for you. There were gas lights in Burscough in 1858.'

My mother stabs her finger at him, 'One night you were at Carlton House. I was in my attic bedroom, and I heard the old bell ring and ring. You told Becky the maid not to let my mother in. I looked out of the attic window. I saw my mother leave down the lane with her head bowed.'

'She weren't family no more! – the smallpox got her.'

My mother says, 'All I wanted was a simple country life.'

'Simple country life! – coal dust, emphysema, damp houses, smallpox, consumption – don't you see what I did for you? – I saved you from all that.'

'I watched my mother walk down the lane, I never saw her again. I watched her go past the hazel tree, then she turned the corner, I never saw her again.'

It was the spring of 1932.

'She got smallpox, you know that, you know that! Look, I worked for you all. I was an engine winder at Jonathan Blundell and Son by the time I was twenty-one. By the age of thirty I'd sunk a nine-hundred yard shaft in India for the Mysore Gold Company. I loved India. It made my fortune.'

'You forced my mother, cold and hungry and ill, to walk back to Hoscar. She was desperate. The greengrocer gave her a lift into Wigan in his van.'

'He never did, it were nothing like that. Sinker Piggott they called me. Sinker Piggott. And I was mayor of Burscough in 1912.'

'My mother went on into the back streets of Wigan.'

'You're dreaming, my girl, you be quiet, you hear. You're just a girl, you never knew. Sinker Piggott they called me – I made you.'

My mother looks into him, 'But I saw the death certificate. Ten years before I died an anonymous person sent me my mother's death certificate.'

'You be quiet, you spoilt bitch – you know nowt.'

Great-grandfather is leaning over me and I feel him spitting at my mother.

My mother continues, 'She died, it said on the death certificate, from the insertion of a blunt instrument into...'

'Smallpox, smallpox, smallpox.'

'You killed my mother – she died from an abortion.'

My great-grandfather sinks to his knees.

He says, 'I'm so sorry, I'm so sorry – I turned your mother away.'

My great-grandfather stretches his hand towards my mother. 'We are both dead, now, but can we ever be at peace?'

My mother turns to me, 'I can be at peace now.' She fades into vapour.

My mother has gone to meet her mother. She passes the hazel tree on the road to Hoscar and sees her mother coming round the lane. They embrace.

A little girl in a ponytail is standing with her mother on Parbold Hill. Amongst the spring flowers they are flying a kite.

JEREMY WORMAN has reviewed for *The Observer*, *The Sunday Telegraph*, *The Spectator*, the *New Statesman*, the *TLS* and many other publications. 'Storm at Galesburg' won the Cinnamon Press Short Story Competition in 2009 and 'Terry' won the Waterstones / *Multi-Storey* competition in 2002. His short stories and poems have been published widely. His first novel *It's All Right, Ma* is with his literary agent Christopher Sinclair-Stevenson. He has degrees in English from London University and Cambridge University and teaches English Literature to American students at Birkbeck. www.jeremyworman.com